THE
WOMBAT
STRATEGY

THE WOMBAT STRATEGY

A Kylie Kendall Mystery

BY CLAIRE MCNAB

alyson books
los angeles

MANUFACTURED IN THE UNITED STATES OF AMERICA.

THIS TRADE PAPERBACK ORIGINAL IS PUBLISHED BY ALYSON PUBLICATIONS,
P.O. BOX 4371, LOS ANGELES, CALIFORNIA 90078-4371.
DISTRIBUTION IN THE UNITED KINGDOM BY TURNAROUND PUBLISHER SERVICES LTD.,
UNIT 3, OLYMPIA TRADING ESTATE, COBURG ROAD, WOOD GREEN,
LONDON N22 6TZ ENGLAND.

FIRST EDITION: MAY 2004

04 05 06 07 08 a 10 9 8 7 6 5 4 3 2 1

ISBN 1-55583-836-7

CREDITS
COVER ILLUSTRATION BY NICK STADLER.
COVER DESIGN BY MATT SAMS.

for Sheila, my muse

ACKNOWLEDGMENTS

Warm thanks to my truly excellent editor, Angela Brown.

ONE

"G'day. I'm Kylie Kendall." I thrust out my hand. "And I reckon you're Ariana Creeling."

The woman seated behind the broad, black desk had pale blond hair pulled back from her still, cool face. I immediately wished I had eyes like hers—icy blue. Mine are boring brown.

She repeated "Kylie Kendall?" as if I'd unexpectedly popped out of a hole in the ground and she had no idea what to do with me. Then she got up and came round to shake my hand, fast and hard. "I'm Ariana Creeling. Again, may I say how sorry I am about your father."

I'd spoken to her once before, when she'd rung from Los Angeles two months ago to say my dad had suddenly died. I'd been shell-shocked by the news, but I could still remember how I liked her American voice. Now that we were face to face, her accent didn't seem quite so strong.

She was older than me, almost as tall, and she needed to put on some weight. Of course, black's slimming, like my mum always tells me, so the fact that Ariana Creeling was wearing black from head to foot—black top, black pants, black high-heeled boots—probably made her look thinner than she really was.

I looked down at myself. Quite a contrast. No one's ever called me skinny, plus I hadn't had time to change from the plane, so I was in jeans and a T-shirt, both a bit grubby. What I wouldn't have given for a hot shower, after twelve hours in a Qantas jet. "I've come straight here from the airport," I said.

"You flew from Australia today? You must be tired." She didn't sound too concerned, but at least she added, "Would you like coffee?"

"Tea? Tea would be great. Black, two sugars."

Ariana picked up the phone and pressed a button. "Melodie?"

I had a fair suspicion she wasn't going to get a reply. "Hope I'm not dobbing someone in," I said, "but there was no one at the front desk. The sign said MELODIE, but Melodie wasn't there. Waited around for a bit, then shoved my suitcase behind the chair and came looking for you."

"I imagine she's off on one of her many auditions." Ariana didn't sound too chuffed about it. "Make yourself comfortable. I'll be back in a moment."

Too restless to sit, I slung my shoulder bag onto a chair, shoved my hands into the pockets of my jeans, and began to stalk around the office. Diffuse light poured in through a skylight, emphasizing the room's white-walled starkness. There was a black desk, its surface bare of anything but a telephone and an onyx desk set. A plain, high-backed chair sat behind it. The filing cabinets were black too. Near the window were two black leather lounge chairs, separated by a white marble coffee table. The floor was dark polished wood accented by a couple of rugs with geometric designs in earth colors. There were a few framed photos on the wall behind the desk, mainly groups of LAPD cops in uniform. It wasn't difficult to pick out Ariana, as she'd scarcely changed from the hard-faced, narrow-eyed cop she'd been when the shots were taken.

She came back with two steaming mugs. "Coasters," she said, indicating with a jerk of her head a pile of them sitting on top of the filing cabinets.

"Right! Coasters." I grabbed two and was heading for the comfort of the lounge chairs when I noticed she was on her way to her seat behind the desk. So that was how it was going to be. I reversed direction, plunking one coaster on her side and one on mine.

I looked suspiciously at the mug she set down in front of me. A tea bag was floating in it, and the smell wasn't what I'd expected. "Is this tea?"

"Herbal."

I inspected the little tag on the string. *BlissMoments,* it said. Jeez...

Waving me to a chair—a spindly thing with a tall back and a sort of black leather sling for a seat—she said, "I'm very surprised to see you here, Ms. Kendall. I had no idea you were visiting the States. If I'd known, I'd have arranged for someone to meet you at the airport."

"Call me Kylie. Everybody does. Sorry to lob in on you like this, but I didn't know I was coming until the other day. Sudden impulse, know what I mean?"

This one looked like she'd never had a sudden impulse in her life, but then again I'd only just met her, so it wasn't fair to judge.

"You're here on vacation?" she asked.

"Business, really." She raised one eyebrow just a fraction, so I added with my best mischievous grin, "To be straight-up with you, I'm here to collect my inheritance."

Crikey, that got a reaction. "Pardon me?" When this sheila frowned, it was like a light went out in her face. "Your visit isn't necessary," she snapped. "My attorney has been in touch with your..." She waved a hand around, searching for the word. I noticed she was wearing a heavy gold signet ring.

"Solicitor," I said helpfully. "That's what they're called in Oz. Bluey Bates. He's the best solicitor in Wollegudgerie. Not hard to be, since he's the only one." She didn't crack a smile at that, so I went on, "Bit of a bush-lawyer, but Bluey's got his head screwed on right. He told me you want to buy the fifty-one percent of Kendall & Creeling my dad left me."

I hadn't believed it when the Los Angeles lawyers had got in touch and said Dad's will gave me a controlling share of his private-eye business, a chunk of money, plus some old car he'd restored.

Ariana's eyes were like twin blue lasers. "I have forty-nine percent, as you know. I need to consolidate in order to run the company effectively. I believe my offer's a fair one. However, I am willing to negotiate—"

She broke off as the phone on the desk shrilled. Excusing herself, she picked up the receiver. "Melodie? Oh—Lonnie. Melodie's not back yet?" She listened, then said, "He's here already?" She checked her watch, a neat gold number. "Give me a couple of minutes, then show him in."

I got up, clutching the mug of pretend-tea. "You'll want me to make myself scarce, then?"

"If you don't mind. I have an appointment with a client. We can continue our conversation later, but I do want you to think over my offer. As I said, it's negotiable."

"Fact is," I said, "I'm thinking about staying in L.A. I was born in the States, and I've got a Yank passport, so no worries about working."

"Working?"

"I know I'll have to do some pretty tough training, but I've never been afraid of hard work. And I've done the self-defense course the Wollegudgerie Police Club put on."

"The Wollegudgerie Police Club?"

I ignored the hint of incredulous amusement in her voice. "Too right," I said. "And I'm not skiting, but I wasn't too bad, if you can believe it. Tossed the captain of 'Gudge's footy team over my shoulder, no trouble."

Ariana didn't look the slightest bit impressed, so I went on, "I'm not a total no-hoper, you know. For one thing, I'm a crack shot with a rifle and fair enough with a shotgun. Never fired a handgun, though. You can't get them in Oz the way you can here."

She was tense as a coiled spring behind her desk. "Why are you telling me this?"

"I'm deadset keen. You won't be sorry."

Her jaw absolutely dropped. "Oh, no, you're not..."

"Yeah," I said, "I'm thinking of becoming a private eye. Like, how hard can it be?"

TWO

As I juggled my shoulder bag and the mug outside in the hall, I caught a glimpse of a man on his way to Ariana's office. He was a big bloke, and he looked vaguely familiar. Not wanting to get into a conversation, I hoofed it down a whitewashed hallway looking for the kitchen. No way could I drink this BlissMoments stuff. Maybe there was some proper tea somewhere. Finding a cactus planted in a tall jar, I poured the contents of my mug around it, figuring something as tough as a cactus could survive even herbal tea.

I had a feeling I was being watched. Sure enough, there was a big, tawny cat sitting in the hallway looking blankly at me. "Hello, cat," I said.

It blinked at me slowly, twitched a whisker in a sneer, then got up and walked off, giving a little flick to its tail as it passed. Even the cat didn't like me.

Out of sight around a corner, I slumped against the wall. Things were grim. My dad was dead before I'd even got to know him. Back in Wollegudgerie was Raylene, the woman I'd believed was The One, but last week she'd given me the heave-ho for someone else. On top of that, Mum was getting married again, and three was going to be a definite crowd. Then on an impulse I'd hopped a plane and traveled to a country I didn't remember from my childhood, to find Ariana Creeling making it very clear I was a lot less than welcome. And to top it all, I was jet-lagged.

I wiped my eyes with the back of my hand and straightened up. So today wasn't the best. I was bloody well not going to let it get me down.

From the little I knew of him, I thought my dad would be disgusted with me for being such a sook. I was guessing about that, because the only chance I'd had to spend any time with him, apart from when I was a really little kid living in Los Angeles, had been a couple of years ago when he'd lobbed into Wollegudgerie and given Mum the shock of her life, because she hadn't thought she'd ever see him again.

The way Mum told it, she'd fallen in love with a visiting Yank who was all man and then some, married him, and moved back to the States to set up house. A year later she had me. Dad joined the LAPD and everything was hunky-dory until he announced he'd realized he was gay and was in love with another bloke—a builder who'd been doing alterations to the house. Dad left the police and started a security business; Mum divorced him and moved back home to the 'Gudge, where she bought the local pub.

Mum always blamed the pollution for Dad turning gay. Said he'd never had ideas like that until they'd lived in the Los Angeles smog for a few years.

Opal mining is Wollegudgerie's main business, which means there's pretty well no pollution, so she couldn't blame the air quality when at 17 I told her I was sure I was gay too. Mum said it was a phase, and I'd grow out of it. I didn't.

Dad paid support for me until I was 16, but the money was sent direct to Mum's bank account. She'd heard nothing from him for years, and he never even remembered my birthdays, so it was quite a surprise when he appeared out of the blue. I'd only seen him in old photographs and wasn't prepared for this handsome stranger who looked a bit like me. I'd gotten my dark hair, brown eyes, and olive skin from my mum, who's part Aboriginal, but now I could see I had my father's nose and hands and height.

Though a bit stunned, Mum was pleased to see him, because, as she said, it wasn't like he'd thrown her over for another woman. She asked him what had happened to Ken, the guy he'd fallen for, and he said they'd lived together until recently, when Ken died. I remember he got tears in his eyes when he said Ken's name.

Anyway, Dad and I got on like a house on fire, straight off. He told me all about the private-eye business, how he'd started Kendall Investigative Services as a loner but then taken in a partner, a woman who'd been a cop in the LAPD, so the company had been renamed Kendall & Creeling Investigative Services.

I was kicking myself now for not ever having asked him if Ariana Creeling was gay, but how was I to know I'd need that information? I'm just not good at the gaydar thing, and the only vibes I'd got from Ariana so far were pretty hostile. Could hardly blame her, with me suddenly turning up to throw a spanner in the works.

After his visit, Dad and I had kept in touch by phone and e-mail. As far as anyone knew, he was in perfect health, but then he'd had a sudden, fatal heart attack. He'd never even hinted that he was leaving me his share of the business, so his will came as a big surprise—but not half the surprise it must have been for Ariana.

I heard someone behind me and turned around. "Hi," said a bloke coming down the hall. He was trying to hide it, but he walked with a slight limp. He'd leave the kind of track in the bush that'd be child's play to follow.

He stared at me with open curiosity, then cocked his head and frowned, probably seeing some family resemblance. "Can I help you?" he asked.

I waved the mug. "Looking for the kitchen."

"Right here." He gave me the once-over. "I'm Lonnie. And you...?"

"Kylie." I gave him the once-over back. He was a little shorter than me and rather chubby, with a roundish face complete with dimples. He had straight, floppy brown hair that fell over one eye, and I'd guess when he was a kid someone had told him he had an adorable smile, because he was giving me a little-boy grin that I had to admit was pretty disarming.

I grinned back at him. "My dad was Colin Kendall."

His smile disappeared. "I'm so sorry. Your father was a great guy. It was terrific working for him."

"What do you do here?"

"The technical side—computers, tuners, scanners, anything electronic. Want to know everything about a certain someone? You come to me. All I need is a name and a social security number and I'll tell you a person's finances, credit rating, driving record, any criminal charges...and that's just the beginning."

"Crikey. What happened to privacy?"

Lonnie laughed like I'd said something funny. "Long gone, honey. Long gone."

I opened a cupboard and gazed hopefully into it. "You think there's any decent tea around here somewhere?"

"The tea bags are right in front of you."

With growing revulsion I examined the brightly colored assortment: dandelion root, peppermint, strawberry, mint, ginseng. Not a genuine tea leaf in the lot. "These are flavored. Beats me how anyone can drink them."

Spooning coffee into a percolator, Lonnie said, "Fifteen minutes, tops, you can have some of this."

I usually don't drink coffee, but I was starting to wilt pretty badly, so a caffeine jolt sounded good. "Right-oh. I'll have a dekko while I'm waiting."

"Dekko?"

"A look around." I frowned at the heavy black wood of the kitchen door. The same as Ariana's office door, it was studded with fat brass buttons. So, I recalled, was the front door. And the building itself, clearly once a house, was a bright sort of pinkish-ocher color. I asked, "Is this place in some sort of particular style?"

"Spanish," said Lonnie, screwing up his face. "Pseudo-Spanish, actually. Very big in Southern California."

He leaned against the counter and crossed his ankles, looking like he was settling in for a long chat. I didn't feel like nattering on, so I said bye and went off exploring.

Finding the back entrance, I stepped out into the glare. This door was plain, made of metal painted dark brown. It was on a spring, and it slammed shut behind me, so I'd have to go around the front to get in again. The sun had a bite. It was late autumn Down Under, so it had to be late spring here. Half the yard was taken by a garage; the rest was filled by a couple of citrus trees—a lemon and a lime—plus a jacaranda, heavy with purple blooms, that hung half over the high back fence. The garage door was locked, and the back gate was barred with metal rods secured by padlocks. Standing on tiptoe, I could see a narrow laneway.

I turned around to survey the house. It sort of squatted there, its thick stucco walls supporting a roof of fat, curved terra-cotta tiles. High up, the dark brown ends of several beams protruded from the walls. There were dark brown shutters on each window, but they were fakes: They looked like they'd just been flung open but were really screwed into the wall as fixtures. Every single window at the back and down the side when I made my way there was barred, like the place was a prison. Good luck if there was a fire inside and you wanted to get out.

On my way along the side of the house I peered through one

window and found the room contained a bed and dresser. Pressing my nose to the glass, I saw the open door of what looked like a bathroom with a shower recess. Right then I imagined what bliss it would be to stand under a spray of hot water.

I made it to the front, where the taxi had dropped me off. "Sunset Boulevard," I'd announced when I'd got in at LAX, a bit thrilled to be saying such a famous name. The driver, a sour bloke with a droopy mustache, twisted round and gave me the hairy eyeball. "Sunset's a long boulevard. Where?" I'd passed him Kendall & Creeling's address, and he just grunted and took off like a startled kangaroo. Never said another word, even though I tried a couple of friendly comments.

What would have been the front garden had been turned into a parking area, then there was a courtyard leading to the entrance of the building. The courtyard had a red terra-cotta floor and a fountain in the middle dribbling water in a half-hearted sort of way.

I wandered around the parking area trying to match a car with Ariana Creeling. The most impressive vehicle was a white Rolls Royce convertible with the license plate DEERDOC. It hadn't been in the lot when I'd arrived, so there was no way it was Ariana's. Actually, I had her pegged for the dark blue BMW. The Beemer wasn't new, but whoever owned it kept it looking sharp.

As I was standing there, feeling totally bushed and in desperate need of that coffee, a bright red convertible came roaring through the gates and nearly skittled me. "Watch it!" I said.

The driver was the missing Melodie. I wasn't psychic. Her license plate said MELODIE and had musical notes dotted all over it.

"Oh, sorry," she said, whipping off her sunglasses and unfolding herself from the cramped driver's seat. "Didn't see you."

I'd thought Ariana a bit on the light side, but this one was famine thin. She had masses of blond hair, high cheekbones, wide green eyes, and teeth so white they reflected sunlight.

"How did the audition go? You ace it?"

Melodie looked startled for a moment, but she didn't mind talking about herself, even if she had no idea who the hell I was. She lugged a huge makeup bag from behind the seat. "Real well," she said. "Going for the second lead. I'll get a call-back, I just know it."

She had a silvery voice to go with her name. And terrific legs—on display, as she was wearing a miniscule skirt and high heels that would've hobbled me permanently. We set off across the parking area, Melodie trotting along quite nimbly, considering her heels, and going on about her audition.

When she paused, I said, "I'm Kylie Kendall."

Melodie flashed me another smile. She seemed to have more teeth than most people. "Hi, Kylie." Then she did a sort of double-take. Halting at the front door of the building, she stared hard at me. "Kendall? Like, Colin Kendall?"

"My dad."

Melodie looked at me more closely. "You're from Australia. That's why you talk funny."

"Too true."

"I've always wanted to go to Australia, but it's such a long way." She tapped her forefinger against her lips thoughtfully. "Although, they *are* making a lot of movies there now." She had a set of perfect fingernails that couldn't be real, painted an odd sort of murky red.

The brass-studded front door opened into a tiled area embellished with more cactus plants in large earthenware pots. Lonnie was sitting behind the reception desk, and he didn't look pleased. "About time," he said to Melodie. "You said you'd be back an hour ago."

"Oh, sorry, but you know how it is." She leaned over and kissed him on the cheek. "You're such a sweetie to cover for me."

He rolled his eyes.

"This could be the one, Lonnie. My big break."

"You say that every time."

"This is different. I nailed the part, I really did. They loved me!"

"You say that every time too."

Melodie gave the kind of airy laugh I've never been able to pull off. "Don't worry, I'll still talk to you when I'm famous," she said.

Lonnie sneezed, then glowered at her. "Julia Roberts has been in my room again."

Melodie turned to me. "My cat," she said. "She loves Lonnie, which is real sad, because Lonnie hates her."

"I don't hate Julia Roberts, I'm allergic to her."

I blinked as it suddenly occurred to me that these two were my employees. After all, I did own fifty-one percent of the company, so fifty-one percent of the staff was mine. "Anyone else work here?" I said.

They both looked at me, obviously wondering why I wanted to know. "There's Bob Verritt," said Lonnie, "and Harriet Porter, part-time."

"And Fran," Melodie added.

I would have asked more, but Lonnie said, "Ariana told me to tell you she'd like to see you in her office."

"Right-oh."

I felt a surge of enthusiasm. Maybe she was warming to the idea of having me as her business partner. I bounded down the hall and flung open her door. The handle slipped out of my hand, the door whacking hard against the white wall. It made quite a racket, so I had the undivided attention of the two people in the room—Ariana and the bloke in the pale gray suit I'd caught a glimpse of before. They were sitting opposite each other in the comfortable chairs.

"Sorry to barge in like this." Jeez, I felt like a galah. I knew I was blushing.

The gray-suited bloke hauled himself out of the depths of the black leather chair. "Ariana's been telling me all about you, Kylie Kendall. When I heard you were a fellow Aussie, I just had to say g'day."

He was quite a specimen—tall, well-built, and handsome in a weather-beaten, squinting-at-the-horizon sort of way. His fair hair was thick, and he wore it in a casual windblown style that probably took quite a lot of effort to get just right.

"G'day," I said back, wondering why I knew his face. A celebrity of some sort? It was L.A., after all. Then it struck me. The DEER-DOC on the white Rolls Royce convertible in the car park was the clue. This was Dr. Dave Deer, famous as the Aussie psychiatrist to the stars.

Dr. Deer was flashing an electric smile. "Maybe you've heard of me," he said. "I'm Dave Deer."

"I may have," I said.

Of course I'd heard of him. The whole of Oz had. Even in remote Wollegudgerie we knew all about Dave Deer's success story—how he'd become a media star in Australia by treating everyone who was anyone when they went bonkers with his Slap! Slap! Get On With It therapy. Then he decided to help superstars overseas. I reckon he'd settled on California as a base because celebrities there seemed to suffer more than ordinary people. And they had money—lots of it.

"Ariana tells me you're thinking of getting involved in the P.I. business."

I slid a glance in her direction. Why would Ariana be telling Dave Deer about my plans? Her face didn't show anything, but she was drumming her fingers on the arm of the chair. Nice hands, I thought.

"Thought I might give it a bash," I said.

"Good on you, mate! Then I'll be seeing you around." Checking his heavy gold watch, he said, "Gotta go. It's patients wall-to-wall this afternoon." He made a rueful face. "And you know how celebrities hate to be kept waiting."

Thinking Dave Deer was a bit up himself, I said, "Is that so?"

"They're not like ordinary mortals, I'm afraid. But they come to me for help, so what can I do?"

I just looked at him. Dave Deer was a *lot* up himself, I decided.

"I'll see you out," said Ariana, shepherding the doctor in the direction of the door. "Be back in a moment," she told me.

My stomach growled. The airline breakfast I'd eaten somewhere off the coast of California was now a distant memory. In fact, the whole flight seemed remote. I put this down to jet lag, smothered a yawn, and decided I really did need a mug of coffee or I'd keel over any minute and fall asleep on the floor.

Ariana came back, and like she'd read my mind, said, "I've told Melodie to order pizza for everyone. That okay with you?"

"Too right! I could eat a horse and chase the rider."

Her lips twitched, just a little. Fair dinkum, one day I might just get a smile out of her. I said, "What's Dave Deer here for? I reckon I can ask, being your partner."

Ariana went behind her desk and sat down. She gave me a long, blue stare. A cold one. She really did have bonzer eyes. "Before I go into that, have you thought a little more about selling out to me? I'm willing to increase my offer substantially."

"I'm not too keen on selling."

I saw a muscle jump in her cheek. She was browned off with me, I could tell, but trying not to show it.

"Los Angeles is thousands of miles from your home," she said, putting emphasis on "thousands."

Home? A vision of my last scene with Raylene flashed in front of me like a movie. It wasn't pleasant—we both said things we shouldn't have. Raylene was a teacher at the local school, and Wollegudgerie being as small as it was, it was deadset I'd run into her all the time. She had pretty well shredded my heart, and I wasn't up for more punishment. What's more, she'd taken up with Maria at 'Gudge's one and only hairdressing salon, so where would I get my hair cut if I stayed?

I shook my head. "I don't think I'll sell my share."

In a reasonable tone, like she was talking to someone pretty dim, Ariana said, "This idea of yours of becoming a private investigator—it's not a piece of cake. It takes real commitment."

"I'll do whatever it takes."

She was making a real effort not to snarl at me. "I'm asking you, before you make a final decision, to sleep on it. Okay?"

"Well, that's the thing," I said. "I haven't got anywhere *to* sleep. Like I told you, I just up and left. Didn't take time to book a hotel or anything."

"You can stay here." She went on to explain how one of the advantages of having offices in a converted house was that a bedroom with adjoining bathroom was available for the odd overnight guest, or for someone who'd been on a stake-out all night and needed a place to get a couple of hours' sleep.

I thanked her, not letting on I'd already scoped out the bedroom through the window, not wanting her to think I was a stickybeak. Then it hit me: Why was I thanking Ariana when half the place was mine?

"Who's Bob Verritt?" I said. "And Harriet Porter? Oh, and Fran?"

I was beginning to expect her answers to be crisp, and she didn't disappoint. "Bob's an experienced P.I. He's out of town on a case. Back tomorrow. Harriet works for us part-time. She's putting herself through law school. Fran does filing, messages, that sort of thing. A general gofer."

"Gofer?"

"Go for this and go for that."

I grinned at her. "Bit like a bitser."

"You have me there."

"What you'd call a mongrel dog—a bitser's a bit of this and a bit of that."

The corners of Ariana's mouth curled just a little. One day I was going to get a full laugh out of her, but I wasn't holding my breath. She said, "I'd strongly advise you to avoid calling Fran a bitser."

"I was commenting on the parallel construction," I said, prim-like. That made her blink, but then, she couldn't know I'd been terrific at English grammar at school.

I found out why Ariana had given that advice about Fran when we all trooped down to the kitchen for pizza. Fran came in last. She was a little thing, a redhead with pale skin and quite a would-you-look-at-that bust that sort of stuck out like a shelf above her narrow waist and, frankly, sexy hips. She would have been quite good-looking but for the nasty scowl on her face.

If my mum had been there she would have given some helpful advice about the danger of creating permanent frown lines and how whistling a happy tune was the way to go. I wasn't that pushy. I just said "G'day, I'm Kylie" and gave her a cheerful smile. Lead by example, my mum always says.

"Fran," she growled in response.

"Don't mind her," said Lonnie, grinning. "She's always like this, aren't you, Sunshine?"

Fran shot him a look that could have dropped a crow clean out of the sky, and stomped over to the counter where unopened pizza boxes were piled, filling the air with mouthwatering smells. Switching her attention to Melodie, she said, "Did you order vegetarian? You *know* I'm a vegetarian."

"I hope so." Melodie was clearly more concerned with her nail polish. "Rats! I got a chip," she announced, holding out a finger for inspection.

Fran mumbled something unpleasant under her breath. I winked at Ariana. "I see what you mean," I said, with a nod toward Fran, who was opening each box in search of a suitable pizza. "She's not a bitser at all. More an attack dog."

Ariana's expression didn't change, but I sensed she was softening a bit toward me. Of course, that was probably wishful thinking. She wanted me long gone. I'd just have to show her how I'd be a dinky-di asset to Kendall & Creeling. Then she'd warm to me.

Or maybe not.

THREE

Full of pizza and with a slug of coffee to keep my eyes open, I went off to have that longed-for shower. Lonnie had kindly brought my battered old suitcase down from the front desk and shown me where the sheets and towels were kept.

My room, at least for tonight, had bright throw rugs on the polished dark flooring, a queen-size bed with an elaborate carved headboard, and a brightly patterned bedspread that matched the curtains. There was a table by the bed and a huge, heavy dresser against one wall. A television set and combination video/DVD player sat on metal shelving, positioned for viewing from the bed.

The place was also something of a storeroom, with a pile of cartons stacked against one wall and a sports corner containing two golf bags with clubs, several tennis rackets, and a tightly rolled exercise mat.

I luxuriated under a very hot shower, washed my hair, and shaved my legs—the last not for any reason except it gave me an excuse to enjoy the spray drumming on my shoulders for a little longer. My hair was short, so it dried quickly. Changed into fresh clothes, and feeling delightfully clean, I thought I'd go back and talk things over with Ariana. But first I'd have a quick lie-down on the bed...

"Wake up, sleeping beauty."

I opened my eyes to Lonnie's cheeky smile. "What time is it?"

"After six. Everyone's gone home, and I'm locking up. Just checking to see you've got everything you need. There's food in the kitchen, so help yourself."

I followed his chubby body to the front door, feeling a little uneasy to be left alone in a strange house in a strange city. Lonnie didn't reassure me much when he said, "You're locked in tight. No one can get in. You should be safe."

"*Should* be?"

He pursed his lips. "Any neighborhood can be dangerous after dark, some more than others."

"Is this a some, or an other?"

He flashed his charming little smile again as he punched me on the arm, gently. "Just be careful, okay? Don't let anyone in, no matter how convincing a story they come up with."

I must have looked a bit alarmed, because he rushed to assure me the outside was floodlit until sunrise, then gave me the number of the security service that checked the building at intervals during the night. "But call the cops if you think there's a real emergency—" He broke off to look over my shoulder. "Don't come near me, Julia Roberts!"

The tawny cat I'd seen before was strolling in our direction, tail held high. "Does Melodie's cat *live* here?" I asked.

Lonnie screwed up his face. "Unfortunately, for the moment, yes. Melodie's between apartments, and staying with a friend where pets aren't allowed." He added in a long-suffering tone, "The fact that I'm violently allergic to cat hair doesn't seem to matter to anyone except me."

Seeing Julia still making a beeline for him, he backed out the front door. "I'm outta here. Sleep well."

After he left, I did a circuit of the building, double-checking things were secure. In Wollegudgerie, most people didn't even bother to lock their front doors. It was different here. I'd seen enough American TV to know an unlocked door was an invitation for some yobbo to come on in.

A quick squiz around the place showed me that not everyone had furnishings as stark as those in Ariana's office. Lonnie's area was so crammed with computers and other electronic thinga-mabobs that there was hardly room to turn around. Bob Verritt's room— I knew it was his from the framed diploma on the wall—was comfortably messy, with files spilling off his desk, an old-style jukebox in one corner, and a wall full of movie posters. One of them, *The Shining,* depicted Jack Nicholson, ax in hand, smiling maniacally through the splintered remains of a door at a screaming female. Crikey, I hoped that wasn't going to be me later on this night. Nah, it wouldn't be: I'd never screamed in my life, not even when my cousin Rob dressed up as the Whinging Lady and popped out of a wardrobe.

"Will you protect me from intruders, Jules?" I asked. She'd been following me from room to room. If cats could shrug, that's what she would have done. Instead she yawned, then froze with eyes wide, like she'd heard something out of the ordinary.

My heart flopped around a bit. "What can you hear?" I whispered, thinking I should have asked Lonnie if there was a gun anywhere. I mean, wouldn't there be firearms in any self-respecting P.I. office?

Julia Roberts waited until I was checking Bob Verritt's desk for some sort of weapon, then she put one back leg in the air and started washing her nethers. Evidently any danger had passed.

I couldn't help feeling she was playing with me. "Caught me once," I told her, "but next time I won't believe you."

I made a quick call home to Wollegudgerie to tell Mum I'd

arrived in one piece. She asked lots of questions, but I said I was tired and would call again later in the week.

In the kitchen I investigated the contents of the refrigerator. Apart from the remains of pizza from lunch, there were the makings of an omelet—eggs and a packet of sliced ham that didn't look too ancient.

"What's half-and-half?" I asked Jules. It appeared to be very runny cream, so I threw a good lot into the bowl with the eggs.

Now that we were in the kitchen, Julia Roberts was acting a lot more friendly. It occurred to me that maybe no one had thought to feed her. I spied a couple of plastic dishes under the table, one with water, the other empty. Jules whipped up enough enthusiasm to speak. Having been brought up with cats, I could translate: "Forget what you're doing. Feed me. Now!"

Fortunately I found tins of cat food in the second cupboard I tried. "Would you like turkey? Or tuna?"

I gave her turkey. It seemed very American to me, and she was, after all, an American cat.

After we'd both eaten we retired to the bedroom. Jules was perceptibly friendlier now that I'd demonstrated my worth. As a companion, she was nice to look at but rather unnerving. She had the habit of fixing her glowing green gaze at the corner of the room, or out the half-open door, as if someone or something were about to appear. I made a mental note to ask tomorrow if the house happened to have a resident ghost.

Personally, I didn't believe in the spirit world, but Mum's pub, the Wombat's Retreat, is supposed to be haunted by the Whinging Woman, dressed all in white, who wanders around complaining loudly and walking through walls. I've never seen her, but there's plenty who say they have—usually booze artists after a session in the bar.

Jet lag might have hit me like a mallet behind the ear this

afternoon, but now that I was ready for bed, in my pajamas and with my teeth cleaned, I was about as wide awake as I could be. Jules and I snuggled up on the bed, the remote between us, to channel-surf.

I paused on *Entertainment Tonight*, not because I particularly watched the program—we got it in the 'Gudge via satellite very early in the morning—but because of the face on the screen. Dr. Dave Deer, leaning nonchalantly on a spade, was in a impressive, well-groomed garden. His gray suit had been replaced with a khaki shirt, brown cord trousers, and working boots. He'd even gone so far as to wear an Aussie Akubra hat.

"G'day," he said to the camera.

The interviewer was a glossy, super-thin woman—naturally—with lots of blond hair and a luminous smile. Cosmetic dentists, I reckoned, had to make a motza in this town.

"We're here in the beautiful Beverly Hills garden of Dr. Dave Deer, famous for his innovative Slap! Slap! Get On With It therapy, which has recently taken L.A. by storm."

"Bonzer to be here on *E.T.*," Dave Deer said.

"Spectacular garden."

"It *is*, isn't it?" Modest grin. "Nature can be very healing."

The blond shook her head, apparently impressed by this insight, then said, "I wonder, Dr. Deer—"

"*Dave*, please!"

"I wonder, Dave, if you'd care to comment on the rumors that your famous clientele include luminaries such as Jim Carrey, Renée Zellweger, controversial Aussie director Jarrod—"

"I must ask you to name no more names! Patient privacy is paramount." Dave Deer looked pleased and indignant, all at once.

"So you wouldn't care to confirm a report that you met with a high member in the current administration—"

"Stone the crows! No comment." Then he added, almost with

a wink, "But I can say everyone here in the States has been very open to new ideas, and that openness goes right to the top. I'm saying nothing more." Then he did wink.

The blond sent a meaningful look to the camera, then swung into her next question. "Is it true, Dave, that patients sign a release that allows you to actually *slap* them?"

"Again, that's confidential."

"What *can* you tell us, Dave?"

"My therapy can help anyone who sincerely wants to reach his or her full potential of happiness and achievement..."

I switched channels as he launched into the spiel he'd perfected back home in Oz. Jeez, if you believed Dr. Dave Deer, it didn't matter whether you were just a touch down in the mouth, or a zonked-out druggie, or straight-out mad as a two-bob watch—Slap! Slap! was the treatment for you.

I knew I shouldn't, but I then watched a horror movie about a bunch of people who insisted on wandering about this creepy old house, even though they were getting gutted one by one. "Doesn't it rot your socks," I said to Jules, "the way they never stick together? Someone's always saying to someone else, 'Wait here, while I investigate,' and then it's curtains for one of them."

After a while, even the shrieking of the victims didn't stop my eyelids from drooping. I hardly had time to punch the off button and turn out the light before I was asleep.

I woke up in the middle of the night, for a moment not sure where I was, but convinced something was wrong. Then it all came back to me with the unwelcome shock of a bucket of water in the face. I'd left Australia in a rush, believing my dad had wanted me to have the business so I'd arrive at Kendall & Creeling and be accepted straight off. It hadn't worked out that way.

Even though I'd closed the curtains tight, enough illumination filtered through from the floodlights outside for me to make out the time when I squinted at my watch. Early hours of the morning here, but back in the 'Gudge it was evening the next day.

It'd be busy in the Wombat. Marge and Sandy would be dishing out beers and smart-alec remarks from behind the bar, and Mum, along with Jack, her husband-to-be, would be chatting up the tourists and joking with the locals.

A sudden shaft of homesickness closed my throat, and I snuffled as my eyes filled. Bloody hell! I wasn't going to lie here and bawl like a crybaby. I *never* cried. I turned on my back, annoying Julia Roberts, who clearly considered the bed her territory. Putting my hands behind my head, I took Mum's advice—be positive, not negative—as I considered the situation.

No one in L.A. would give a brass razoo that Raylene and I had split up. Not so at home, where everybody took a keen interest in everybody else's business. And some people would pity me, and I *hated* that.

Besides, if I stayed in Wollegudgerie, there wasn't much in the career line for me. I'd grown up in the pub, and when I was old enough, helped Mum run the place. It was me who installed an up-to-date computer system to keep track of the business, and me who persuaded Mum to let me organize a Web site to suck in the tourists.

But when Mum told me she was going to marry Jack O'Connell, I knew I couldn't stay. Don't get me wrong, Jack's nice, but he likes to think himself the boss, and after years of being my own boss there was no way I was going to be happy having him tell me, a twenty-eight-year-old sheila, what to do, particularly when I probably know the business a lot better than he does.

Even before the news about Dad's will, I'd been thinking of moving to the big smoke, probably Sydney. So why not Los Angeles instead?

Still, I should have researched what you did to become a private investigator in California. I'd ask Ariana tomorrow. Was there an exam? I'd always been good at them. Or maybe I could take some P.I. course online.

In spite of some bird outside who was running through a set of complicated vocal exercises, I drifted back into a half-sleep, thinking of online courses I'd taken. Mum had got me to take Advanced First Aid. She said it was a good idea to be prepared in case there was a particularly nasty fight in the bar one Saturday, always the worst night of the week for aggro.

Then I researched adult education sites run by various colleges and universities and decided on astronomy. In the Outback the stars are dazzling, because they aren't drowned by city lights. I bought a telescope from a catalog and enrolled in Astronomy I and II. For something different, I'd followed that with Conversational Italian, which I was practicing on Maria in the hairdressing salon. How was I to know she had her eye on Raylene, and worse, that Raylene had her eye on Maria?

I must have thrashed around a bit at this thought, because Julia Roberts started to complain. "Fair crack of the whip, Jules," I said to her. "You've got nothing to whinge about. You've got looks, a home, and people who love you."

That plunged me into further gloomy musings, and I'd almost decided to get up and make myself a cuppa—before I remembered there wasn't any decent tea in the place—when I slid into sleep again. The last thing I thought of was Ariana's blue eyes. And the fact that she wanted me gone—and I wasn't going.

The next thing, I was waking up to the sound of someone moving around outside in the hallway.

It seemed barely daylight, so I shot out of bed ready to confront the intruder. Looking around for a weapon, I spotted the sports stuff in the corner. I settled on a golf club. Julia Roberts was still curled up on the bed but roused herself to give me an odd look as I barefooted it toward the door, nine-iron raised for action.

I wasn't feeling brave, but I had no intention of cowering in the room, so I bounded out into the hallway thinking I'd have the advantage of surprise.

And surprise I did. The little bloke I confronted gave a shriek, dropped the wastepaper basket he'd been holding, and put up his hands to protect his head.

"No! No!" he cried, following that with a stream of words I didn't understand. They sounded vaguely like Italian, and I made a guess and said, "Spanish?"

"Si." He stared at me rather like the cat had a minute before. I had to look like a complete dingbat, standing there in my pajamas with a golf club.

"Sorry," I said, dropping my arm so he could see that I wasn't going to bash his brains in. "You're the cleaner?"

He nodded warily. "The cleaner," he repeated. Without taking his eyes from me, he took a step back.

"G'day," I said in an effort to make him feel I wasn't a threat. "I'm Kylie. Kylie Kendall."

"Kendall." He nodded and took another step backwards. This was embarrassing. I could just see Ariana Creeling's frosty expression when she found out I'd terrorized the cleaner.

"I'll just get dressed," I said, and beat it back to my room.

I kept out of the cleaner's way, and he certainly kept out of mine. I heard the buzz of a vacuum cleaner, but it didn't come near my door, which I'd left wide open to prove I wasn't lurking behind it.

At about eight Ariana appeared in the doorway. "Luis tells me you threatened him with a golf club."

"How was I to know the cleaner came in at dawn? No one told me."

She paused to consider this. "You're right. Someone should have."

"Breakfast?" I said hopefully.

"I picked up a box of Krispy Kreme doughnuts on my way here."

Yerks! Doughnuts at this time of morning?

"I'm used to eating porridge every morning."

"We might have some instant stuff."

Instant porridge? My stomach rumbled. If I had to, I supposed I could eat it.

I followed Ariana to the kitchen, admiring her loose-hipped stride. All in black again, she wore tight leather pants. I wondered who she went home to. No one as attractive as she was would be alone...although she did seem to be a bit of a cold fish.

Lonnie had coffee on and was already chomping his way through a noxious yellow doughnut. Behind him pictures danced on a TV set, although the sound was muted.

"Put whatever you need on the list," Ariana said, indicating with her coffee mug a magnet notepad stuck to the fridge door. "Fran usually stocks the kitchen once a week, but you can write 'Urgent' next to an item and she'll get it that day."

I carefully printed *loose tea (NO flavors)* and *URGENT*. "And I don't suppose you have a teapot, either," I said to Lonnie, who was licking his fingers after swallowing the last of his doughnut.

"Ask Melodie," he said as she breezed into the room.

"Ask me what?"

"Teapot," said Lonnie, selecting another doughnut. "Kylie wants to know if we have one."

"Nope."

"Put it on the list," Ariana said over her shoulder on her way out of the kitchen. "And when you're ready, Kylie, come to my office."

Melodie had her long, blond hair up today, twisted into a sort of knot and skewered by a tortoiseshell comb. It should have looked untidy, or at least as if the whole arrangement was about to come down, but on her it gave a casual, stylish impression.

"Did Julia Roberts behave herself?" she asked.

"She was okay, but she kept on staring into space. Gave me the willies. This place isn't haunted, is it?"

"Haunted?" Lonnie chortled. "Probably rats in the foundation, or maybe a family of skunks. I'll set up sensors, if you like, to catch your ghost."

Melodie sent him a quelling look, then said to me, "Julia Roberts is very sensitive." She gave her perfect teeth an airing. "Or she could have been teasing you."

"We've got a ghost at the Wombat's Retreat," I said. When they both looked blank, I explained, "The pub my mum owns, back in Wollegudgerie."

"What's a wombat?" Lonnie asked.

I was used to explaining this to foreign tourists. "An Aussie marsupial, a tough little animal that digs burrows wherever it takes its fancy. No good trying to stop them—they're like furry steamrollers when they get their minds set on something."

I dug out a key ring from the pocket of my jeans. "This is what a wombat looks like." It had been my idea to have Wombat's Retreat key rings made as publicity for the pub, and it gave me a pang to see it in my hand, so far away from home.

"Sort of like a bear," said Melodie. "Would a wombat attack you?"

"No, but it might walk over you if you got in its way."

"Australia's got such cute animals," Melodie enthused. "I just *love* those cuddly koala bears. And *birds*. My aunt's got one of those big white cockatoos with the yellow crests."

"That reminds me," I said. "There was this bird in the middle of the night. Whatever it was, it had a real routine of clicking sounds, and trills, and snatches of birdsong. When it got to the end, there'd be a break, and then it'd start all over again."

"Mockingbird," said Lonnie. "They arrive here in spring and drive everyone mad for a couple of months." He wiggled his eyebrows at me. "Trying to attract the ladies, that's what they're doing. Each of them has his own individual song."

A man I presumed was Bob Verritt stuck his head through the kitchen door. "Lonnie, there's a messenger at the front with a package for you. Something from Dr. Deer." He caught sight of the carton. "Any left?" Then he caught sight of me. "Hello!" He came all the way into the kitchen. "So you're Colin's daughter. I'm Bob Verritt."

He was one of those very tall, thin, concave guys who are sort of curved over themselves. His blue suit hung on him like his shoulders had been replaced by a wire hanger. He had lank hair of no particular color, a long face with a beaky nose, and the nicest smile. He even had a chipped front tooth, which was a first for the dentally perfect people around here.

He seemed surprised when I put out my hand, but he shook it anyway, saying, "I can't tell you how sorry I am about your father. He was a regular guy."

"Thanks. I wish I could have known him better, spent more time with him."

"You take after Colin in one way—he could rattle Ariana's cage too."

"She's upset?"

That got a hearty laugh. "And then some. She's just told me how you dropped in out of the blue yesterday and have plans to stay. All I can say is when I left her office, she wasn't a happy camper."

"Whoa," said Lonnie. "If Ariana's on the warpath, I'm getting out of the way."

"Don't forget, the messenger's waiting," said Melodie.

Lonnie didn't seem in much of a hurry, wandering off with a mug of coffee and yet another doughnut.

Melodie turned her wide green eyes on me. "How come you've upset Ariana?"

Bob Verritt answered for me. "Kylie's aiming to become a P.I. and replace her dad in the business."

"No!" Melodie looked at me with admiration. "But it's so hard. And you'll have to get a green card and everything."

"I don't need a green card," I said. "I was born in Los Angeles. I'm an American citizen."

"I thought you were Australian." Melodie spoke in the reproachful tone of someone who'd been fooled. "You sound like one."

"I'm an Australian too. I've got dual citizenship."

"Cool!"

Something she'd said hit me. "What do you mean it's hard to become a P.I.?"

Bob said, "You haven't been a cop, have you? Or got a degree in law or criminology."

"That's a no to both."

"Well, since you're starting from scratch, after the FBI says you haven't got a criminal history, you have to put in three years as a trainee under the supervision of a licensed P.I."

"Crikey! Three years? I was hoping I'd just have to take some sort of exam."

My disillusionment seemed to amuse Bob. "The exam's after you've completed a total of six thousand hours—two thousand each year. And you have to be paid for your time, or it doesn't count."

This was turning out to be a bigger commitment than I'd bargained for. "Let me get this straight. I'm an apprentice for three years, then I take an exam, then I'm a true-blue P.I.? Right?"

"Unless you've got a criminal record."

Hoping my disappointment didn't show, as I hated it when anyone felt sorry for me, I grinned at him. "No record. They never caught me."

"I auditioned for a P.I. role once," said Melodie. "One of three girls working for this millionaire. *Guy's Eyes,* it was called. Glad I didn't get the part. The show never made it past the pilot episode."

"Major bummer," I said, being polite. *Three years* was buzzing around in my head. But hell's bells, I didn't have any concrete plans for the future. I could start off, and if I didn't finish, well, that was the way it went.

It suddenly occurred to me that Ariana could stonker me completely by refusing to be my supervisor. "You're a licensed P.I., aren't you?" I said to Bob.

He put up his hands. "Oh, no, Kylie. I'm not going to be the meat in the sandwich between you and Ariana. Work it out with her."

"I'll do that."

No time like the present, as my mum always says. I'd need my strength, so I grabbed a plain doughnut and washed it down with coffee. Then I strode down the hall to Ariana's office, set on following yet another of my mum's pieces of advice: Start as you mean to continue. I was going to start off confident, sure of myself. Ariana would be begging to take me on as a trainee.

The door was open and Ariana was behind her desk, her blond head bent over something she was reading. "Got a mo?" I said.

She skewered me with her blue gaze. "Sure."

I felt my self-confidence leaking away a bit. Maybe I should chat her up first, approach the subject from the side, burble on for a minute or two about nothing in particular.

"Yes?" Ariana said.

"I want you to be my supervisor. Bob Verritt's explained the whole P.I. thing. I know about the three years and all that." When she continued to look at me, expressionless, I added hastily, "I'm really keen, dinkum I am. You won't be sorry."

"I get inquiries almost every week from individuals who think it would be great to be a private investigator. I tell them all the same thing: It's not enough to want the job. You have to have the skills."

I couldn't think of any particular skill that would help me here, so I said, trying not to sound defensive, "I'm interested in people. What makes them tick." Jeez, did that sound like I might be a bit of a stalker? "But I'm not what you'd call a real sticky-beak, so no worries there."

Ariana sighed. "Okay, Kylie, I'll ask you the questions I use for would-be interns."

I sat up straight. "Fire away."

She didn't look enthusiastic. "Do you have computer skills?"

"Yes."

That took her back a bit. "You do?"

I took a minute to detail how I'd set up the pub's system and how I'd learned a lot of different programs—word processing, accounting, home office printing, and so on. And then I remembered the courses I'd done, so I told her about them.

It seemed to me Ariana had perked up a little. "How about photography? Any experience?"

"Back home, I've got my own darkroom." Now I was sounding up myself, just like Dave Deer. "Look, I'm not claiming to be a crash-hot photographer of people, which is probably what you're looking for. All my shots are of wildlife, or landscapes."

She asked me a few questions about cameras, and I must have answered okay, because she nodded. She said, "I don't suppose you're familiar with digital cameras?"

"I brought one with me. Got it as a Chrissie present last year." I didn't add it had been a gift from Raylene and I'd seriously considered leaving it behind. But hell, it wasn't the camera's fault that she'd turned out to be two-faced.

Ariana's expression had gone from blank to maybe-considering.
"You won't be sorry," I said again.
"I think I probably will be."
I jumped to my feet. "Leaping lizards! You're taking me on!"
"Oh, God," said Ariana to herself, but I heard it clearly. "What have I done?"

FOUR

Figuring I'd better learn the ropes, I started off at the reception desk. Melodie was in residence, consuming what had to be the last available doughnut. I eyed it covetously, as my success with Ariana had sparked my appetite.

"What did you think of Dave Deer?" Melodie asked.

"How did you know I'd met him?"

Melodie gave me a knowing smile. "First rule any P.I. should learn: Ask the receptionist. We know everything that's going on."

She didn't seem to notice when I turned the question around. "What do *you* think of Dave Deer?"

Melodie took a white-toothed snap at the doughnut. It was, I noticed, dripping with chocolate icing. Chocolate's one of my weaknesses. "I went out with him once," she said indistinctly.

Now this was interesting. Ariana still hadn't told me what Deer had been doing in her office yesterday, and in the excitement of discussing what I'd be paid and confusing stuff like health insurance and social security, I'd forgotten to ask her.

"You only went out with him once?"

She swallowed the last of the doughnut. "My acting. Dave wasn't all that interested."

I folded my arms and sat on the edge of the desk. "No? That's a surprise."

"I can't date anyone who isn't supportive of my career. I mean, it's a jungle out there. Do you have any idea how many hicks bus into L.A. every day expecting to be discovered?"

"How many?"

Melodie frowned at me. "A real lot," she said. "Every audition's a zoo."

"When do you hear about yesterday's audition?"

"I haven't even got a call-back yet. That reminds me, I've got to get hold of Larry and see if he's heard anything." She added with a hint of satisfaction, "My agent. Larry Argent. That's the first step in an acting career. You've got to have an agent, and they don't take just anyone. You have to have talent, looks, and," she gave me an intense stare, "that star quality..."

"So no probs for you, Melodie."

This got me an indulgent laugh. "You're so cute!" She sobered. "There's a million would-bes with talent and looks and star quality. You gotta have luck too. Be seen by the right people." She sighed. "It's real hard work, I can tell you."

I'd opened my mouth to ask what reason Dave Deer would have to be a client of Kendall & Creeling when Fran, her expression dark, came into view. "You write this? About the tea?" She flapped the list in my face.

"That would be me."

"You're asking for a teapot."

Melodie watched with interest as Fran looked me up and down. "A teapot," Fran repeated. "A teapot? What's wrong with tea bags?"

"Can't live without a teapot. And I forgot to ask for a tea-strainer too, please."

Fran cocked her head at me and smiled a truly cynical smile. "Let me get this straight. You want me to get a teapot and a tea-strainer?"

36

"Yes, please. And tea. A packet of the loose stuff. And make it fair dinkum tea, not those yucky tea bags with flavors."

"Hey," said Melodie, "when I'm stressed after an audition, black currant tea is just about the only thing that can calm me down."

Fran rolled her eyes. "Stressed? Give me a break."

"Could I add something to the list?" I asked.

"And that would be? Russian caviar? Truffles, maybe?"

She reminded me strongly of my Aunt Millie, who's as sour as a lemon and has a line in sarcasm that could wrinkle paint.

"Porridge," I said. "And not the flavored sort—"

"Yadda yadda yadda."

"I beg your pardon?"

Fran made an elaborate act out of adding porridge to the list. "Satisfied?"

"This is just *bonzer* of you, Fran," I said, with the warmest smile I could manage. "I'm ever so grateful." I continued to grin at her benevolently.

My Pollyanna act was practically guaranteed to irritate most people, and Fran was no exception. "Oh, Jesus," she said. "I'm gone." She paused at the entrance to say to Melodie, "Dentist first, then shopping. Don't expect me before lunch." She slammed the door behind her.

"I suppose you wonder how Fran keeps her job," said Melodie.

"It had crossed my mind."

"She's Ariana's sister's daughter."

Ariana had a sister? I found myself deeply interested and was about to ask a few questions when Bob Verritt interrupted with, "Melodie, I've got an urgent integrity check. The client's getting antsy. You can take Fran along."

"No can do. Fran's at the dentist."

"Again? She's as bad as you."

"Cosmetic dentistry's an art," said Melodie, clearly stung by his comment. "It can't be rushed."

"I suppose you'll have to take Lonnie, then."

I piped up, "I can go instead of Fran."

Bob looked me over. "You'll have to change your top. That T-shirt won't hide the camera lens."

"Good as done."

Melodie laughed. "You don't have a clue what this is about, do you?"

"Not a clue. But I'm here to learn the ropes."

"Excellent," said Bob, although I could tell he had reservations. That made me a bit niggly. I'd show him I was a quick learner.

Half an hour later, Melodie and I were getting into her little convertible. Naturally I headed off to the wrong side because I expected the steering wheel to be on the right, where it would be in Oz.

"We drive on the other side of the road in Australia," I said as I went round to the passenger seat.

"That must be real strange."

Melodie leaped in, started the engine, shoved it into reverse, and stamped on the accelerator in one continuous movement. We shot out backwards onto Sunset Boulevard, were narrowly missed by a bus, and then zoomed forward, all before I could get my seat belt fastened.

The traffic was, well, unbelievable. I'd had a taste of it in the taxi yesterday, but this morning it seemed even worse. I couldn't remember even the cousin of a traffic jam in the 'Gudge, except once when our footy team won the Country Challenge Cup for the first, and probably only, time. Here in L.A. there seemed to be a zillion vehicles driven by people all busting to get somewhere fast.

We drove along Sunset, with me twisting my neck around to see all the sights and memorize street names. We turned right at Fairfax and picked up a bit of speed. Melodie was singing along with a golden-oldies radio station as the wind whipped her blond hair behind her like something out of a shampoo ad. Mine, being shorter, just churned around on my head.

I had to admire the way she drove, zipping her sports car around larger vehicles and into tiny gaps, leaving blaring horns behind her. "There's a lot of four-wheel drives," I observed.

"Four-wheel drives?" When I pointed at one, she got what I meant. "We call them sport utility vehicles, SUV for short."

"Don't you ever signal?" I asked after she changed lanes for the umpteenth time.

Melodie broke off in the middle of the chorus of "Pretty Woman"—it was hardly fair she could sing, on top of her looks—to say, "What for?"

"Oh, I don't know. So other drivers would have some idea what you were going to do, maybe?"

"They know," said Melodie. "No one's run into us yet, have they?"

"Crikey, a few were close."

"Ah!" Melodie swiveled her hand around in a gesture I presumed meant I shouldn't get my undies in a knot.

Without warning she suddenly turned the wheel and we shot into a crammed parking area fronting a shabby row of little shops. "That's the one."

CARDSHARP CARDS announced the sign above the door.

Melodie had taken the lone parking spot, snaffling it from a bloke in an old Yank tank, who'd been approaching from the other end of the lot in a cloud of gray exhaust. He screeched to a halt behind us, leaned out, and went completely off his nana.

"I'll set that hoon straight," I said, reaching for the door handle. Melodie grabbed my arm. "No hassles. "We're on a job, remember? Besides, he could have a gun."

The bloke yelled a final insult, then took off. As practice for my budding career in private investigation, I memorized his plate number, then got out to survey the scene. Cardsharp Cards was jammed between a fast-food chicken place and a frozen yogurt shop. This wasn't a bustling shopping area; the activity was provided by a few stray bits of paper blowing around. A shopping cart piled with odds and ends was abandoned near the Cardsharp entrance. I suddenly realized what I'd taken to be an untidy bundle of clothes next to it was actually a person sitting on the ground, smoking. It was a woman, not old, but thin and withered, as though most of the moisture had been sucked out of her.

The door of Cardsharp Cards was wrenched open and a man in shirtsleeves came out. "Get outta here!" he bellowed at the woman at his feet. "And take your motherfucking cart with you." He kicked it so it slewed around, narrowly missing her.

"That's Eddie," said Melodie, glancing at the photograph his wife had provided. "A regular sweetheart."

I'd had a crash course in integrity tests from Lonnie while he wired me up. Basically, Melodie was to tempt this guy, to see if he could be trusted to stay on the straight and narrow.

Eddie, hands on hips, was glaring at the woman, who'd made no attempt to get up. "You've got ten seconds," he ground out, "and then..." He drew back his foot, obviously aiming to kick *her* this time. "One, two, three..."

The woman scrambled to her feet, spat on the ground near Eddie's shoe, then took the shopping cart and trundled away slowly, stopping every now and then to look back at Eddie with a sneer. He waited until she'd disappeared around a corner, dusted his hands, and went back into his shop.

"Let's get him," I said, all fired up.

Melodie, who'd changed into a tight, glittery top and slapped on lots of makeup before we left, said, "Follow me in after a minute or so, but check your equipment first."

I had a miniature video camera clipped to my belt and hidden under my favorite pink hibiscus shirt. The lens and microphone, attached to the camera by a thin wire, were both so tiny they fitted into a buttonhole.

Lonnie had showed me how to operate the camera, reminding me to always make sure that my chest was pointing in the right direction and that nothing would muffle the microphone or obscure the lens.

Hoping the microphone wouldn't pick up my racing heart (I was a bit nervous, this being my first real job), I pushed open the Cardsharp door, trying to look like an ordinary person in search of a greeting card. I tripped over the SAY IT WITH A CARD! doormat, but the man behind the counter didn't notice—his attention was all on Melodie. I could see why. Melodie was walking with a swinging hip movement that had him hypnotized.

Trying not to breathe too heavily, as I didn't want the picture to be jerky, I made my way along a display of greeting cards. This was harder than I thought, keeping my chest pointed in the right direction while I seemingly surveyed the contents of the racks.

Eddie ran a hand over his slicked-back hair, licked his lips, and stepped from behind the counter. He was a reasonably good-looking bloke, if you liked the flashy sort. "And how can I help you, pretty lady?"

"I'm looking for love and friendship cards." There was a break in Melodie's voice, and her lips trembled.

Eddie's expression was all warm concern. "If you don't mind me saying so, you seem upset."

"It's nothing." Brave smile. "You know, I'll never understand men—how they think."

"Boyfriend trouble?"

Melodie batted her eyelashes. "How did you know?"

Eddie spread his hands. "In the card business, you learn to be sensitive to these things."

"We've had a fight. I thought a card..." I could almost see tears in her eyes. "Todd says it's over, but it can't be."

"Todd must be a fool. A beautiful woman like you!"

"Thank you," Melodie breathed.

"I'm Eddie."

"Melodie."

"What a lovely name."

I got a bit closer, hoping to get a clear recording of their conversation.

Melodie gazed up at him. "Thank you, again."

Eddie shook his head. "I know just how you feel, Melodie. My girlfriend and I just broke up."

"You're not married? All the nice ones are taken, I've found."

"Not *this* nice one," Eddie declared. "I haven't met the right girl"—meaningful pause—"yet."

I managed to turn my snort into a sneeze. Eddie glanced in my direction. I picked up a card and examined it closely. His attention snapped back to Melodie.

Touching her lightly on the arm, Eddie said, "You know, it's the loneliness that gets to me, know what I mean?" A moment, then he added, "Even in a crowd, I can feel so isolated, so alone."

Jeez, this was vomit-making.

Melodie nodded a sad agreement. "It's so hard to trust again."

Eddie took her hand. "We're both in the same boat, you and me. I wonder if you'd like a drink, maybe something to eat, somewhere nice."

"You're asking me on a date?"

"Why not? We're both free. And you shouldn't let one bad experience sour you on life."

"I'm not sure..."

Eddie practically melted with sincerity. "Fate has brought us together, Melodie. We shouldn't waste the opportunity we've been given."

"I don't know...it's so soon..."

"At least give me your number."

She shook her head. "I'll call you. Tomorrow, perhaps."

A flicker of annoyance on Eddie's face was quickly replaced with an understanding smile. He handed her a business card. "You can call me here, at the shop. Or on my cell. The number's there."

"Not at home?" Melodie purred. "I love to have sexy conversations, don't you? When we're both in bed and on the phone..."

Thinking fast, Eddie said, "There's a problem with my home phone—the whole street's out."

"You know, Eddie," said Melodie, "I don't know if I'm all that interested."

"Please, Melodie, I'd love to take you out. We'll have fun together." There was a pleasing note of desperation in his voice as he saw his chances slipping away.

Melodie mused for a moment. "I'll think about it, Eddie, but don't hold your breath."

His expression as he watched her sexy walk out the door was half randy and half angry resentment. With pleasure I delivered a final blow. "Mate," I said on my way out, "your cards aren't much chop. Pitiful, really. Wonder to me you stay in business."

Melodie was waiting for me in the car. "His wife was right. Her Eddie's an asshole."

I grinned at her, pleased that I'd done my part without a hitch. "A regular bull artist," I agreed.

Then my smile went south as I remembered that I wasn't the only deceived one around. Being half a world away from Raylene hadn't helped at all. If I didn't want to get all weepy again, I had to get mad.

"What's the matter?" asked Melodie, starting the engine. "You've got a funny look on your face."

"It's my killing look."

Melodie started to laugh, then broke off to peer at me. "Stop it," she said, "you're scaring me."

FIVE

On the way back we took a detour to some special vegetarian place to pick up lunch. It took some time, as there was a long queue. Melodie, still in her temptress outfit, collected scads of attention from the blokes around. She didn't seem to mind, though, flashing her smile in all directions. "You never know who you'll see," she said in a confidential tone. "People in the biz often come here."

"What's the biz?"

She gave me a look of kindly scorn. "The entertainment business," she said in explanation. "The biz. You'll have to learn all about it if you're going to succeed in this town."

So far today I'd only had one doughnut for fuel, so I ordered up big when I made it to the counter. I had some trouble working out the American money when I paid.

"How come your bank notes all look the same?" I asked Melodie as we walked back to her car.

"You mean bills. And they're not the same." She stopped to take out a couple for my inspection. "See, they're different."

"But they're pretty well all the same color."

"Are you saying Australia's got colored money?"

"Blood oath, it has. Every denomination is different, and—"

"Aaaagh!" Melodie galloped off as fast as her high heels and tight skirt would allow. "I'm here! I'm here!" she called.

Her words were directed at a very large woman in a too-small uniform standing next to Melodie's convertible. When I came up, I heard the woman say in a satisfied tone, "Meter's expired."

Melodie clasped her hands for all the world like she was begging for her life. "Oh, please," she said. "Don't write me a ticket. I'm positive I put in enough quarters. Something must be wrong with the meter."

The woman tapped the offending meter. "Expired," she said. Then she made a big deal of checking the license plate and jotting it down on the gizmo she was holding.

Melodie wasn't giving up. "I can't have been more than a minute or two over. Oh, please. I got a ticket last week, and I can't afford to pay that one. And now..." Her shoulders drooped.

"Standing at an expired meter." This dame was having fun, I could tell.

"I'm begging you not to write me a ticket."

There was a sob in Melodie's voice. It was so convincing I decided maybe she did have a career in acting.

"Once I've started a ticket, can't stop. Regulations." She slapped the ticket into Melodie's hand. "Have a nice day."

"Damn!" Melodie said once we were in the car. "If it had been a guy, I'd have talked my way out of it. I've gotten away with it thousands of times."

When we drove into the office parking area, I felt a little thrill to read the name on the wall beside the gate. KENDALL & CREELING INVESTIGATIVE SERVICES. I couldn't claim the Kendall part referred to me. Not yet. I made a silent promise to myself I'd be able one day to point to it and say, "P.I. Kylie Kendall at your service."

"What the hell kept you?" demanded Lonnie from the reception desk. "I've been stuck here for hours answering the phones." A lock of his hair had fallen over one eye, and he looked quite endearing, rather like a plump toy.

While Melodie soothed Lonnie, I took the salads we'd bought down to the kitchen. I would have loved a cuppa, but there was no tea, no teapot, no strainer, and no Fran. I looked around for something to drink. A large water cooler brooded in one corner, and the fridge was full of bottled water, plus many cans of Diet Coke.

There was a rustle of plastic bags, and Fran tottered in. "You and your teapot," she snapped. "Had to search high and low, I can tell you."

"Is there something wrong with the tap water?" I inquired. "Doesn't anyone drink it?"

Before I could help, Fran had made her way across the kitchen and swung the shopping bags onto the counter. It must be a trial to be so short, I thought, looking at her diminutive form.

She answered my question in a withering tone. "Nobody *I* know drinks water from the faucet." Vinegary smile. "You can be the first."

I was fast getting the irrits with Fran and was ready to have it out with her right there and then, but a strange woman, who captured my attention entirely, chose that moment to come into the kitchen.

"Hi," she said. "You must be Kylie. I'm Harriet. Harriet Porter."

"G'day."

This one was a bit of all right. She had a honeyed contralto voice, a warm smile that crinkled the corners of her eyes, thick chestnut hair, and, for a change, she wasn't anorexic. Harriet Porter was one of those people who give the instant impression they're true blue. What you saw was what you got. At least I hoped so, as even in a severe business suit this was the sexiest woman I'd met for some time.

"Ariana tells me you're joining us as an intern," Harriet said. "Welcome aboard."

"I'm giving it a go."

Fran, noisily unpacking her bags, said, "You'd better be a quick study. Ariana's not famous for her patience."

"If Kylie's anything like her dad, she'll do just fine," said Harriet. To me, she added, "Colin was such a terrific guy. It's hard to believe he won't walk through the door any minute. Please accept my deepest sympathy for your loss."

"Here," said Fran, shoving a brown pottery teapot into my hands. "This what you ordered?"

Considering the way she'd snarled at me this morning, it was astonishing she'd come up with anything, but here was exactly what I wanted.

"Absolutely," I said, examining it. "Thank you, Fran."

"Strainer and tea." Fran dumped the items on the counter in front of me. She rummaged around and added a box with an illustration of a family ecstatic over breakfast. "And porridge. I figured you meant oatmeal. Too bad if you didn't, because that's what I got."

"Your blood's worth bottling, Fran." She grunted, but not with malice. Being friendly, I added, "You're Ariana's niece, aren't you?"

That got me a narrow look, like she thought I was needling her. "What's it to you?"

Harriet put an arm around Fran's shoulders and gave her a squeeze. "Lighten up, Fran. Kylie's just interested."

Astonishingly, Fran smiled. Grudgingly, to be sure, but it was a dinkum smile. Perfect teeth, naturally. "Yes," said Fran, almost pleasant. "My mom's Ariana's eldest sister."

This was the nicest I'd ever seen Fran. Harriet could obviously work marvels. Or maybe she and Fran... I dismissed that thought. My gaydar might be dodgy, but it wasn't that off.

"Fran's mom is an artist," said Harriet. "A very successful one, I might add. She's got an exhibition coming up, hasn't she, Fran?"

Fran, quite animated for her, nodded. "A gallery in Santa Monica."

"Do we all get invites?" I asked.

Fran's scowl reappeared. "The private showing's for selected guests." It was clear from her expression I had a snowball's chance of being one of these.

"Stone the crows! I wasn't trying to jump the queue."

Ariana's cool voice came from the doorway. "I didn't know you were interested in art, Kylie. If you're really keen, you can come to Janette's private showing with me."

"You're on."

"No big hurry, but after lunch I'd like to go through a few things with you."

"Right-oh."

Ariana poured herself coffee and left the room. I made a pot of tea, drank two cups black, with lots of sugar—I had to search for the sugar, as everyone else seemed to use artificial sweeteners—chomped through my salad, and then choofed off to Ariana's office.

"Dave Deer," I said before she could bring up anything else. "You never told me what he was doing here yesterday."

"It's a highly confidential matter."

"I won't be blabbing to anyone."

She gave me one of her long blue stares. "Dr. Deer has his consulting room set up to make discreet audiovisual records of each session with his patients. The individual disks are meticulously catalogued and put in the appropriate files, which are stored in a walk-in safe."

I could see where this was going. "A not-so-secure safe, is that it?"

She nodded. "Several disks are missing. They haven't been misplaced, as all the patients' records have been checked."

"Blackmail?"

Ariana leaned back and regarded me with a genuine smile. It was only a tiny one, but definitely more than a twitch of the lips. "Very good, Kylie. Blackmail it is. Two patients have session disks missing: Bart Toller, who's an up-and-coming actor, and Jarrod Perkins, who's—"

"The Aussie film director," I finished for her.

Jarrod Perkins had started off his career in Australia with a horror movie called *The Dead! The Dead!* I'd never forgotten it, because it had scared the living daylights out of me when I'd seen it at the Regal in Wollegudgerie. A couple of minutes into the story and I'd stopped noticing the spring in my seat digging into me, or that Raylene was holding my hand. Even the yobbos up the back of the cinema shut up when the body pieces started flying and the blood really began to flow.

That movie became a cult thing, and it made it overseas, so Perkins got larger budgets for his next movies. Soon Oz was too small for him, and he hit Hollywood in a big way with a weird musical called *Shitstirrers' Spring*, although I'd heard in the States it was advertised as *S***stirrers' Spring*.

In an interview on *Entertainment Tonight* Jarrod Perkins got all het-up and yelled, "What the shit is wrong with *Shitstirrers' Spring* as a name?" I remember reading he got his knickers in a real knot when it was broadcast as: "What the BLEEP is wrong with *BLEEPstirrers' Spring* as a name?"

"So what's happening?" I asked.

"Yesterday a letter came through the mail claiming to have the material from the files and indicating a large sum of money will be required for the return of the audiovisuals. No specific sum was mentioned. This was the first anyone knew anything was missing."

I'd seen enough blackmail stories to know what to ask next. "Who could have got to the files?"

Ariana gave an exasperated click with her tongue. "That's the point. Before this happened, security was slapdash. The door to the walk-in safe was frequently left open during the day."

"You're looking at an inside job, then?"

Again, Ariana almost smiled. "Nice use of P.I. lingo. And, yes. Almost certainly someone in the organization."

"Dave Deer didn't call the cops, did he? Too much publicity."

"Exactly. He can't afford to have his celebrity clients learn their deepest, darkest secrets may not be safely locked away. If this got out, he could kiss his successful practice goodbye."

"I reckon Jarrod Perkins is screaming blue murder."

"Mr. Perkins doesn't know anything about it." Her tone was neutral, so I couldn't tell if she approved or disapproved.

"Blimey. What if he gets a blackmail letter direct?"

With a wry quirk of her lips, she said, "I imagine things will get very interesting."

I was finding her mouth very interesting. Hell, I was finding all of Ariana interesting. And a few minutes ago I'd set eyes on Harriet Porter and thought she was crash-hot, too. All this so soon after Raylene had mashed my heart.

Was I fickle? Not so, I decided. This was a search for an antidote to the pain Raylene had inflicted. Then I had a little smile to myself: I could rationalize anything.

"Something amusing?"

I became aware Ariana was contemplating me with raised eyebrows. "Oh, sorry. Off with the fairies for a minute." I put on my best grave, paying-attention look.

Picking up her phone, she said, "Dave Deer sent over a demo disk of his Slap! Slap! technique as background for our investigation." She punched in a couple of numbers. "Lonnie? Ten minutes. I want to see the Deer demonstration disk. Get Harriet in too. Okay?"

She got up in one fluid movement. Harriet might be super-sexy, but Ariana was fascinating, in an unsettling sort of way. "Come with me," she said, walking into the hall. I puppy-dogged after her.

"This was Colin's office." She opened the door just down from hers. I remembered this room from my security patrol last night. It'd been the only one with wall-to-wall carpet—a charcoal-gray color. The furnishings were pretty spartan—a lighter gray metal desk, with matching bookcase and filing cabinets. There was a flat-screen computer on the desk. A small pile of cartons sat on the floor. As there were no identifying photos on the wall, I hadn't known until now that it had been my father's office.

Ariana pointed to the cartons. "I packed Colin's things away, figuring I'd be sending them on to you." She opened the top drawer of the desk. "I was going to package this separately."

It was a framed photograph of me and Dad I'd never seen before. It had to have been taken in L.A., before my parents broke up. The background was a suburban garden. Dad was sitting on the grass with me, a little girl, standing within the circle of his arms. I was squinting into the camera because of the bright sunshine. In the photo he was looking at me with such affection that seeing it now, my eyes filled with tears. I stood the photo up on the desk, took out my hanky, and blew my nose. "Dust," I said.

"This can be your office."

"I get my own office?"

Ariana seemed mildly amused. "There's a problem?

"No prob, but won't the others think I've got a bit of a swelled head, having this when I'm only a trainee?"

"You need the tools to be a P.I., and a space you can use as a base is one of them. Another is a car. You can't exist in L.A.

without one. For surveillance you don't want a vehicle that people remember, and you certainly must avoid anything that looks like a police car. A four-door sedan in a dark shade would be perfect."

"I've already got a car. Dad left me his, but I don't know where it's kept."

There was an odd pause, then Ariana said, "In the garage at the back."

"Good-oh. Then I'll drive that."

Ariana blanched a little. "That car was your father's pride and joy. It's a fully restored classic Mustang."

I had no idea what that was, but her tone said it was something special. "Gears or automatic?" I asked.

"Stick shift, I'm afraid." Ariana seemed pleased to tell me this. "You'll be needing an automatic. You don't want the distraction of changing gears while you're driving in an unfamiliar city."

"Not just that—it's also the other side of the road to what I'm used to."

Her expression showed she thought the matter was settled. "That's all the more reason why a stick shift's a bad idea."

"I'll see how I go. It was Dad's car, after all. Driving it will make me feel a bit closer to him, I reckon."

Plainly Ariana wasn't delighted. "What color is it, by the way?" I asked her.

"Red."

"You beaut! Never had a red car."

"It's not a color I'd recommend for surveillance."

"What did my dad drive when he was on a job?"

"He borrowed my car or used a rental."

"Can't I do that too?"

Ariana sighed. "We can discuss this later."

On the way to Lonnie's room, she said to me, "If at any time you change your mind, my offer's still on the table."

I opened my mouth to say I'd never change my mind but then shut it again. For all I knew, I might find being a P.I. wasn't all it was cracked up to be. Maybe I'd be pleased to sell out. "Fair enough," I said. "If I change my mind, you'll be the first to know."

Lonnie had an alcove in his work area set up for viewing, which was a good thing, as there was hardly any clear space anywhere else. Harriet was already in place, head bent over a textbook. "Got an exam tomorrow," she said in explanation. "Torts."

"Everyone who sees this demo has to sign a confidentiality agreement," said Lonnie, passing Ariana a clipboard.

I was curious to see the others' signatures, so I made sure I got it last. Ariana Creeling's name was in clear angular script; Lonnie's was a long scrawl with a couple of dots floating above it; Harriet had scribbled her initials.

I began to read the document.

"Kylie, what's taking you so long?" Lonnie demanded.

"I never sign anything till I know what it is."

"It's the standard form," said Lonnie. I didn't look at him, but he sounded like he was rolling his eyes.

Harriet hadn't even glanced at the form before she initialed it, but she still rushed in to defend me. "I think it very wise to read a document before signing."

"Finished." I handed the clipboard back to Lonnie.

"Okay," he said, punching a button. "This is the demo sent to therapists committed to buying a Slap! Slap! franchise from Deerdoc Enterprises."

It started with a blare of classical music, followed by warnings of dire consequences if any portion of the following program were to be copied or viewed by unauthorized persons. Then Dr. Dave Deer himself appeared in a white coat, which nicely set off his tan.

"What you are about to view," he intoned, "is a demonstration of my innovative therapy, Slap! Slap! Get On With It. I must emphasize this is a *simulation*. The patient is an actor. His responses are an amalgam of those most often encountered in a real-life session. That said, the technique itself is exactly as used with genuine patients, with the proviso that slight adjustments may be necessary to suit the specific needs of individuals."

The view switched to a white-and-black windowless room. The thick carpet and ceiling were white; the walls and sparse furniture were black. On one wall hung a large flat-screen TV. There were two straight-back chairs facing each other in the center of the room. An uncomfortable-looking couch was placed diagonally across one corner.

In voice-over Dave Deer said, "Black and white, the essential noncolors, and also the absolutes, provide a paradigm of the patient's worldview. During therapy, the illuminating realization—white and black combine to make shades of gray—will flower in the patient's essential inner self."

I thought I heard Ariana snort, but when I glanced her way her face was blank.

The picture now showed the room with Dr. Deer in his starched white medical coat and the actor playing the patient seated facing each other. "You will note the patient has a clear view of the screen," Dave Deer commented in voice-over, "and I, sitting in the opposite chair, have my back to it. This arrangement of the chairs is vital."

The actor playing the patient was a hollow-cheeked,

intense sort of bloke with dark, burning eyes behind little oval-shaped specs. He wriggled around a bit in psychological agony. "Doctor, I'm deeply troubled." Pause. "Deeply, deeply troubled."

"Don't lose your day job," Lonnie advised the actor.

Dr. Deer's face was impassive. "You're deeply troubled," he agreed. "Deeply, deeply troubled."

The patient nodded. "Deeply. I have fame, fortune, but inside I'm empty. A husk of a man."

"You have fame, fortune, but inside you're a husk of a man. An empty husk."

Harriet hooted. "Who wrote this dialogue? I could do better myself."

The patient opened his mouth to speak but was transfixed by the screen behind Deer's head, upon which had appeared in block letters: DON'T COME THE RAW PRAWN WITH ME. I smothered a laugh.

"What's that for?" the patient said.

The screen went blank. Dr. Deer looked behind him, then back at the patient. "There's nothing there. Do you believe you saw something?"

"There were words up there on the wall. Something about a prawn."

Dr. Deer had another look. "I don't see anything. Possibly an electronic malfunction..." He gave the patient a meaningful stare. "Or a projection of your troubled, inner child."

SOOKS NEVER PROSPER.

"There it is again!" exclaimed the patient. "What's a sook?"

I answered him. "A crybaby."

The words had obligingly disappeared by the time Dr. Deer looked over his shoulder. "Have you had hallucinations before?" he asked.

Harriet said, "What's coming the raw prawn?"

"Aussie slang," I told her. "Means don't try to trick me, slip something past me, like putting a raw prawn in with all the cooked ones."

Dr. Deer's patient was becoming more and more agitated and didn't cope well when NO HIDE, NO CHRISSIE BOX appeared.

The bloke leapt to his feet, screaming, "Look at the motherfucking wall! And don't tell me I'm seeing things!"

The action froze, and Dave Deer's voice-over remarked, "You will note these Australian colloquial sayings, presented to the patient, have a function something akin to Zen koans, which challenge the audience to make sense of nonsense. The patient's struggle to discern meaning facilitates the development of a potential that dwells in all of us—that is, the perception of true selfdom."

A close-up of the patient's contorted face, caught in mid bellow, appeared. "Note the frustration, the lack of control, the almost childlike behavior of the patient," said Dr. Deer. "This marks the seminal, the determining, the shaping point of my therapy."

The frozen picture jerked into life. The patient, spluttering with rage, confronted his therapist, still sitting relaxed on his chair. "I've paid a small fortune for this...for this..."

As words failed him, Dr. Deer stood, drew himself to his full height, slapped the patient very hard on one cheek, then backhanded him equally hard on the other, while saying in a loud, commanding voice, "Slap! Slap! Get on with it!"

"You hit me! You physically assaulted me!"

Dr. Deer smiled, warmly, compassionately. "Your terminology is faulty. What you experienced was not assault. It was, in fact, an enlightening, freeing, clinically controlled, physical gestalt."

"Say what?"

Deer bent to pick up the patient's specs, which had been sent flying at the first hearty slap. "How do you feel?" he asked solicitously, handing them over. "What thoughts are arising from your deepest, innermost, most profound self?"

"That you're an asshole."

Dr. Deer beamed. "Excellent. Your healing process has begun."

SIX

As the screen went blank, Lonnie said, "I know I'm going to be sorry I asked, but what does 'No hide, no Chrissie box' mean?"

"It's a bit complicated," I said. "See, the day after Christmas is Boxing Day. In England it was the day the lord and lady of the manor came around to give food and other goodies to the peasants. See? They handed out Chrissie boxes."

"I'm already sorry I asked," said Lonnie.

"You've lost me," said Harriet. "What's this to do with hiding?"

"Not hiding. *Having* a hide. Like a rhinoceros. You, know, being thick-skinned, so you don't get discouraged easily."

They looked at me blankly. This was uphill work. "Okay," I said, "here it is in a nutshell. If you're not pushy, you don't get a reward. Got it? No hide, no Chrissie box."

"Then I guess you get a lot of Chrissie boxes, Kylie," said Lonnie with a grin.

"Let's get on with it," said Ariana.

Her cool voice got Lonnie moving fast. He rapidly handed out stapled pages to Ariana, Harriet, and me. "This is a staff list, including social security numbers, for Deerdoc Enterprises in L.A. Thirty people are either on the payroll now or were recently employed by Deerdoc."

His look of disapproval plain, Lonnie went on, "Before these people were employed, there were very cursory background checks, or in some cases none at all." He squinched up his face as though in pain. "I keep asking myself, when will they ever learn?"

Ariana said, "We need to dig a great deal deeper."

"You've got that right. Harriet, you take the first fifteen, I'll take the last. There are some Australian nationals, and we could have some difficulty with them because most of their personal information will be in that country."

"The usual info?" Harriet asked.

Ariana nodded. "Contact previous employers and anyone who gave personal references. Look for criminal arrests and convictions, property transactions, credit ratings, bankruptcies, any involvement in civil cases, including divorce. And double-check educational qualifications, especially for anyone claiming a medical degree. We all know how often people lie about their credentials."

A telephone rang. Lonnie had to hunt around to find the handset under the stuff he had piled on top of his desk. "It's Dave Deer for you, Ariana."

"Tell Melodie I'll take the call in my office." She beckoned to me to come with her.

On the way down the hall, I said, "I wouldn't be all that keen on being slapped across the face, specially by a big bloke like Dave Deer. It's a wonder that any of his patients come back for more."

"They come back, all right. He has no trouble keeping his clientele. In fact, he's so much in demand, new patients can expect to wait months for a first appointment."

"You mean if someone like Nicole Kidman rang Dave Deer and said she'd go stark raving mad unless he saw her right away, he'd tell her, 'Sorry Nic, no can do?'"

"I imagine he'd take Nicole Kidman without delay," she said dryly.

In her office, she motioned for me to take a seat as she picked up the receiver. "Dave, it's Ariana." She listened calmly as he spoke. Even from where I was sitting I could pick up on the agitated tone in his voice.

"You're absolutely right," said Ariana. "We have to be proactive. We should meet." She listened. "Yes, excellent. Your house at eight."

An idea was rocketing around in my head. Ariana'd probably give it the big thumbs-down, but like my mum says, you don't know it's a goer till you give it a go.

As soon as Ariana put down the receiver, I rushed in with it. "I've been thinking, nobody knows me at Deerdoc Enterprises except Dr. Deer himself. And Lonnie said there were other Aussies there. So why couldn't I go in undercover? I could suss out the place, no worries."

I half expected I'd finally get a laugh out of her, but it wouldn't be the sort I'd enjoy. That didn't happen. She regarded me thoughtfully, smoothing her pale hair with one hand. This was the first edgy gesture I'd seen her make, apart from drumming her fingers yesterday when I said I was set on becoming a P.I.

At last she spoke. "Maybe that's not a bad idea." There was another long pause while she thought some more, then she said, "I'll call Dave Deer back and tell him you're coming with me tonight, and I'll run the idea past him. It's for dinner, so don't ruin your appetite beforehand."

With a ghost of a grin, she added, "That is, if you're available..."

"Oh, I'm available."

⊃

"For actors, the right name is vital," Melodie advised. She paused to answer a call, then went on, as though nothing had interrupted, "Yours, for instance, would be a good one."

"What? Kylie Kendall? You're joking."

I'd come up front to the reception area to ask Melodie if there was an iron around, as I had to make something in my sparse wardrobe look presentable for dinner at the Deers' place.

"Of course, I had to change mine."

"Your name's not Melodie?"

She frowned. "Not the Melodie, the Schultz. Now I ask you, does Melodie Schultz make you think *star*?"

I had to admit it didn't.

"So I took Davenport as my professional name. How do you think that sounds? Melodie Davenport?" She paused as if listening for an echo.

"Ripper name," I said. When she looked at me with doubt, I went on, "Like, it's absolutely excellent."

Julia Roberts, who had been curled up in a tight ball on the reception desk, pleased me by waking up, stretching, and coming over to be adored.

"She likes you," said Melodie. "Julia's real choosy, so you should be flattered." Then she was back on topic, clearly into deep musing over monikers. "Julia Roberts is a terrific name, but Bob Verritt couldn't be a success in the biz with his. The Bob's the problem. If he used Robert, he might make it. And Lonnie Moore? No way. Not that he's star material in any case."

Another call came through. "Kendall & Creeling...I'll put you through to Mr. Verritt." That done, Melodie moved onto Harriet Porter, commenting that although Harriet was an old-fashioned name, it might be okay, being as there weren't that many Harriets in competition.

I put my search for an iron on hold, and asked, "What do you think of Ariana Creeling as a name? Got possibilities?"

Melodie wrinkled her nose, managing to look attractive doing it. "Don't like the Creeling."

"It's not her married name, is it?"

My casual question earned a casual shrug. "No idea."

Did that mean Ariana was married, or that Melodie didn't know one way or the other? "You mean you don't know if she's married or not?"

"Maybe she has been, maybe not. She's a very private person. All I can tell you is she lives in the Hollywood Hills. I've been to her place. It's lovely. Got a great view."

Someone took this moment to dial Kendall & Creeling's number. Melodie glared at the phone. "Look, people, it's Friday afternoon. Give me a break."

This call turned out to be much more welcome, as it was from one of Melodie's friends. Before she and Tiffany could get too deeply into plans for the weekend, I interrupted with, "I'm looking for an iron. Any ideas where I might find one?"

"Hold on," she said to Tiffany. Melodie then gave me the bad news. "You'll have to ask Fran. She's the only one who'll know."

つ

In the BMW, Ariana and I went west along Sunset toward Beverly Hills. Sunset Boulevard was obviously the place to be on Friday night. Twin streams of cars, many of the occupants shouting and tooting, clogged the roadway. The footpaths were crowded with people walking, talking, and standing in queues to get into places. Several of the billboards lining the road didn't just sit there, they scintillated and flashed and boomed with music and sound effects.

Ariana drove the way I expected: smoothly, competently, and with patience. This last quality I admired, not having all that much of it myself.

"That's the House of Blues," she said, gesturing to an awkward-looking building on the left. I didn't have the faintest what the House of Blues was, but I said "Right" as if I did. It was clear to me I needed a crash course on this sort of stuff if I was ever to get anywhere as a P.I. I resolved to quiz Melodie about Sunset nightlife and so on, working on the principle that she'd certainly be in the know.

We swept around a corner and down a hill, and abruptly everything changed. Gone were the crowds, the gesturing motorists, the gaudy lights. A discreet sign indicated that we were entering Beverly Hills. The traffic jams disappeared as the roadway widened. Vehicles sped along, minding nobody's business but their own. I caught glimpses of large houses and luxurious gardens behind concealing walls.

After we'd driven a couple of kilometers, Ariana turned right off Sunset and onto a narrow, winding street. Houses crowded both sides, but no one was out walking the dog or taking an evening stroll. Because there were hardly any streetlights and lots of trees, it was a bit like driving through a leafy tunnel.

I glanced over at Ariana. Illuminated by the lights from the dash, her profile was serene, but I reckoned that inside she couldn't be. "This case is really important, isn't it?" I said.

"Every case is important."

"Fair go, you know what I mean. Dave Deer's a big shot. If things go wrong, he'll cut up rough. It'll be our fault, not his."

She glanced over at me. "What makes you say that?"

"Back in Oz, before he ever came to the States, there was this big fuss when one of Dave Deer's patients, a TV personality, used a shotgun to murder his wife and his mother, then blew himself away. The word got out that in therapy sessions—some with Dave Deer and some with another therapist who worked for him—the bloke had talked about what he was planning, but nothing was done about it. For a while it looked like Dave Deer was in for it, but then, all at once it was entirely the other doctor's fault and Dr. Deer was totally off the hook."

"What are you saying?"

"I'm saying if things go down the gurgler, Dr. Deer won't get sucked in. It'll be someone else's fault, never his. And if he has to blame Kendall & Creeling, trust me, he will."

"Thanks for the warning."

I got the impression she wasn't taking my advice all that seriously, and that made me bring up something that'd been nagging at me since she'd agreed to let me get involved in the case. "I want it straight, Ariana. Are you going to recommend to Dave Deer I go undercover just so you can get me out of your hair?"

She gave an amused snort. "It'd be a lot easier to take you for a one-way ride to the Angeles National Forest."

While I was deciding how to reply to this, she took a sharp right, then a sharp left. Turning into a driveway, we pulled up at fancy wrought-iron gates. Tall walls stretched off on either side. The gates looked substantial enough to stop a tank. I noticed a movement at the top of one gatepost, as a camera swiveled around to stare at us.

Ariana slid down her window, and when a disembodied voice asked for identification, said, "Ariana Creeling and Kylie Kendall. Dr. Deer's expecting us." I liked the way she said my name. Her American accent made it sound exotic.

Silently, in a mega-spooky manner, the massive gates swung open. I twisted around to look back as we went up the driveway. They were swinging closed behind us. "What if the power goes out?"

I didn't need to explain. Ariana said, "I imagine there's a manual release. Besides, my guess is there'll be an emergency generator up at the house."

I guessed she was right. The place was a mansion and a half.

After the darkness of the streets, the huge house was so bright it hurt the eyeballs. There were two stories, laid out in an "E" plan with the center part facing us. Every window of every room appeared to be lit. The entrance area was so brightly illuminated it seemed more like a stage set than anything else. Three shallow steps led up to a front door that had to have been snaffled from a castle somewhere. This enormous door was framed by two columns, each with lots of fussy stonework at the top. Lighting fixtures looking like gigantic, swollen lanterns were set into the wall on either side.

"Crikey," I said. Then I shut up. I didn't want Ariana to think I was a little bushie who'd never been close-up to anything like this in her life.

It wouldn't have been a surprise if a butler in full uniform had opened the door, but instead it was Dave Deer himself. He was dressed in what I'd call upmarket casual. His fair hair gleamed, his teeth gleamed, the gold watch he was wearing gleamed. I felt dull beside him.

"Come in, Ariana. Kylie, delightful to see you again."

Inside the door there were more columns, ornately carved, bracketing the entrance into the main part of the house. Our feet clacked on the parquet flooring. I was wearing heels tonight, not too high, and my best dress, plain and a sort of plum color. Fran, after a pause to whinge, had dug up an iron, and I'd unpacked everything and had an orgy of ironing to make my clothes presentable.

Ariana—surprise—was wearing a black skirt and frothy black blouse. I figured if I had her coloring, I'd wear black too. The contrast made her blond hair blonder, her blue eyes bluer.

A woman in a short, lacy dress came down the curving stairs, like she'd been cued to appear. Dave Deer said, "My wife, Elise. Elise, you know Ariana, of course. And this is Kylie Kendall."

I already knew he was married to Elise Patterson. She was an Aussie and had been a professional tennis player—good but not top-ten material. The best ranking she'd had, I recalled, was somewhere in the low twenties. A few years ago, with her tennis career on the way down, she'd met and married Dave Deer. They'd had a big society wedding in Sydney that'd been splashed over all the popular magazines and made the front pages of most newspapers.

Elise wasn't blond—I'd say her husband wouldn't want the competition—but mid-brown with red highlights. And she was really friendly, taking my arm and leading me through an arched doorway into a living room that dwarfed the furniture and all of us.

"Big, isn't it?" Elise said, as I gazed around the room. Seeing me look up at the two heavy chandeliers suspended from the ornate gold-painted ceiling, she laughed. "I always think the buggers will come crashing down, but so far they haven't."

We had drinks and chit-chat seated on two red couches placed on a fluffy white carpet that floated in a sea of parquet flooring. Between the couches a low table had a huge marble ball balanced in the middle as decoration.

The conversation turned to the likelihood of a major earthquake giving L.A. a good shake-up. Apparently there'd been a couple of minor quakes the week before I arrived, and this had got "the big one," as Ariana called it, on the agenda. "Do you get any warning before an earthquake happens?" I asked hopefully.

When everyone agreed such disasters struck out of the blue, I spent the next few minutes waiting for the chandeliers poised above us to fall or the marble ball to roll off the table and squash someone's foot.

A maid, dressed in a black dress and white apron, just like in some old movie, came in to say dinner was served. We all got up and headed out the arched doorway, which I noticed also had columns, these ones painted gold. As I passed the maid I said "G'day." She gave me a funny look. "Good evening, madam."

"We're in the smaller of the two dining rooms," said Elise.

The other one must have been humongous, as this dining room was pretty big. A wall of glass looked out over a swimming pool. Underwater lighting turned it into a glowing blue-green rectangle.

At one end of the room was a fireplace with a highly wrought metal screen. I hid a smile at the portrait above the mantle, an oil painting of Dr. Dave Deer himself, gazing self-importantly out of the heavy gold frame.

"Don't blame me for the decor," Elise said once we were seated at a large glass-topped dining table with metal legs and black metal chairs padded with cushions embroidered in gold and black. "We're renting this place, fully furnished. I wanted something somewhat less grand, but Dave insisted," she sent him an indulgent smile, "we needed room to entertain."

"Speaking of entertaining," he said, beaming, "we're having a party tomorrow night. I know it's short notice, but Elise and I would love to have you both attend. And of course, bring a guest if you wish."

"Thank you," said Ariana. "I'll come alone."

I wasn't sure whether Ariana would want me at the Deers' party, but when everyone looked my way I had to say something. "Sounds bonzer to me."

The maid, accompanied by a twin of herself also in black with a white apron, came in with the first course, a complicated salad with slices of smoked salmon. The first sip from my wineglass widened my eyes—this wasn't bad plonk at all. In fact, I had to admit it was pretty good.

"An excellent Australian wine," said Dave Deer. "Perhaps you recognize it, Kylie."

Oh, sure, like I'd ever have the money to buy top-of-the-line stuff. "Chardonnay," I said. "Margaret River area of Western Australia?" I'd cheated, of course. Having ripper eyesight, I'd read the district on the bottle's label.

"Very good." He looked impressed.

I felt embarrassed to have fooled him, so I said, "I didn't really know. I read the label."

Instead of being offended, he was amused. "You'll find honesty isn't always the best policy, Kylie."

"Dave and I have been talking about the idea of you going undercover at Deerdoc," Elise said to me. "We think it might work. We've got a cover story. You're to be my cousin, looking for a temporary job while you're in L.A. On Monday Dave's going to tell his assistant to take a couple of weeks' vacation, so you can fill in for her."

"Kylie can't be seen to be associated with Kendall & Creeling," said Ariana.

"We've thought of that," said Dave Deer. "Kylie can move in here with us. That's what Elise's cousin would do, if she existed." He sent a toothy grin my way. "We've got plenty of room, I assure you."

I felt a pang of alarm. Had Dave Deer always had a shark's smile?

SEVEN

After Ariana dropped me off, I did my security rounds, had a shower, and then Julia Roberts and I had a good night's sleep. I only woke briefly when Jules had a full wash at three o'clock. By eight in the morning I was dressed, well breakfasted with porridge and tea, and had studied a street directory called the Thomas Guide. I was ready to brave the streets of Los Angeles.

Ariana had mentioned that both Lonnie and Harriet would be in later. Even though it was Saturday, background checks on Deerdoc staff had to be finished. She said she'd be in the office by eight-fifteen to show me the ins and outs of the Mustang. True to form, she was there on the dot.

Ariana opened the garage, and I saw the car she'd called my father's pride and joy. No way did its vibrant red self look almost 40 years old. Ariana stood with her hand resting on the hood, rather like she was soothing some thoroughbred animal, as she explained how she'd turned the engine over every week or so to keep the battery charged. Then she drove the Mustang out into the lane and painstakingly took me through everything she thought I should know.

I was impatient to get going. I undertook to keep chanting "Keep right! Keep right!" to override my natural tendency to veer left. Ariana wished me luck in a tone that indicated she believed

I'd be needing it. I took off slowly, careful not to kangaroo hop down the lane, the engine rumbling with the promise of thrilling acceleration. Glancing in the mirror, I saw Ariana watching. I had a fair idea she had her fingers crossed. It was obvious she admired the Mustang but harbored severe doubts about me driving it.

Turning off Sunset onto Laurel Canyon, I let her rip in a minor way, enjoying the wind in my face—I had the windows down—and the feeling that somehow Dad was watching me and he approved of me driving his car. My concentration didn't lapse. I admonished myself to keep to the right. I didn't crunch the gears or run into anything. The red Mustang obediently climbed to the top of the canyon road, then hastened down the other side into a suburb I remembered from the directory was called Studio City. How exciting to be driving around the movie capital of the world!

It was awfully disconcerting to have the oncoming traffic on the left-hand side of the road, but after a while I congratulated myself that I was getting used to it.

I had some idea where I might get on one of the many free-ways criss-crossing Los Angeles. Until I experienced the rush of joining that headlong stream of vehicles, I couldn't with any truth say I'd driven in L.A. It seemed a good omen when, after swooping down into the Valley, I found the 101 freeway on-ramp without difficulty.

In a mo I was whizzing along with the rest of the cars. The traffic was light, which I attributed to the possibility most peo-ple in L.A. were sleeping in this Saturday morning. I was think-ing we were all moving well, but not particularly fast, until I remembered with a jolt the speedo was showing miles per hour, not kilometers. It didn't take long for me to find I belonged to the tiny minority in L.A. who used indicators. For everyone else it was all swoop and dive and—surprise!—I'm changing lanes.

This was fun. Daringly, I zipped into the fast lane, which would have been the slow lane in Australia. The Mustang was a glistening red bullet, and I was sure there were admiring glances coming my way.

Things were hunky-dory until I decided to exit the freeway and try the challenge of surface streets again. An off-ramp was coming up, so I zoomed down it, full of confidence. I'd aced this driving-in-L.A. routine, I was telling myself as I approached the intersection of the off-ramp and a suburban street. The traffic light was green, so I attempted the tricky double task of making a left turn, plus changing down a gear at the same time.

Yerks! Like any Aussie at home would, I sailed onto the left side of the road. Only stayed there a few meters until, thanks to blaring horns and flashing headlights, I realized what I'd done. I swerved back to the correct side. It was pure luck I didn't hit anyone, and I was congratulating myself a miss was as good as a mile, when I heard the siren.

Fair dinkum, I got the works from the cop in the patrol car— lights flashing, siren screaming, and then a *woop-woop* sound, plus his magnified voice booming "Pull over, driver."

I obeyed, all the while cursing myself for being a bit of a lair. I felt my face burn with embarrassment. Ariana had been right, and although I was fairly sure she wouldn't say "I told you so," I was damn sure she'd be thinking it.

As if she were beside me, I heard her last bit of advice before I'd taken off: "If you're pulled over, Kylie, keep your hands in plain view. The cops in this town tend to shoot first and ask questions later."

I'd laughed then. I wasn't laughing now. Still, I might just talk my way out of this sticky situation. Glancing in the mirror, I saw the cop get out of his car. He approached slowly, deliberately, paused to check out the plate at the rear, then came to the driver's window.

"G'day," I said, with a subdued smile. "Lovely day, isn't it?"

The cop was wearing the sort of dark glasses that reflect everything back at you, so I couldn't see his eyes. He hitched his belt, which was hung with multiple items, including, I saw with a prickle of alarm, a very deadly-looking gun.

He said, "License."

I fished around for my wallet, found my Aussie driving license, and handed it to him. He examined it closely, his expression perfectly blank. The odds I'd wriggle out of this one didn't look good. Still, it was worth a try.

"Crook photo." I indicated the license he was holding in this meaty fingers. "Makes me look like I'm dead on a slab, don't you think?"

"Residents of California are required to have a California license."

Before I could stop myself, I protested, "Fair crack of the whip, officer. Like, I've only been in the States two days!"

No change of expression. Could he possibly be a robot? The cop turned his head slowly to check out the location of my wrongdoing, then just as slowly swiveled it back my way again. That settled it: He *was* a robot. He said in a monotone, "You exited the freeway and turned onto the left side of the road."

Well, that was stating the obvious. I hastened to explain. "Blame jet lag. Flew in from Australia the day before yesterday. In Oz we drive on the other side, so I'm afraid I got a bit confused. No harm done, fortunately."

He ignored the hopeful don't-book-me-officer look I sent him. Plainly a man—or robot—of few words, he said, "Proof of ownership? Insurance?"

I dimly recalled Ariana mentioning insurance stuff was in the glove box. "You won't shoot me, will you, if I open the glove box?"

No response. Taking that for a pledge not to use deadly force, I rummaged around and discovered a flat wallet containing official-looking papers. I handed it to him, saying, "Actually, it's not my car—"

"Please step out of the vehicle."

Appalled, I stared at him. "You're not going to frisk me, are you?"

I'd seen enough TV cop dramas to visualize this mortifying process. Worse, since I'd been pulled over, the occupants of passing cars had been slowing down to have a look. They'd really have something to see if I got patted down while spread-eagled in an undignified position.

The cop barked, "Exit the vehicle."

I made one last try. "You're not going to book me, are you?"

He put his hand on his gun. That was enough for me. I got out of the car.

⊃

"So then what happened?" asked Lonnie through a mouthful of ham sandwich. He, Harriet, and I were in the kitchen, which I was coming to recognize as the beating heart of the office.

I was feeling a bit rattled, having driven so carefully on the way back to Kendall & Creeling that I'd been tooted by several impatient drivers, and one had even yelled unkind comments about my relatives as he passed me. Even more depressing, I'd gotten lost several times and had to ask for directions.

I gave a squeeze to Julia Roberts, who I'd enticed to sit on my lap to comfort me after my ordeal. "So I get out of the car, and the cop asks me if I've had anything to drink, and I say, no, not unless he counts two cups of tea and a glass of orange juice."

"Good one," said Harriet.

"Unfortunately the bloke didn't have much of a sense of humor."

"Did he frisk you?" Lonnie's tone showed his strong hope I'd be answering in the affirmative.

"No. He just booked me."

"Moving violation," said Harriet.

"Traffic school," said Lonnie.

"What's traffic school?"

Lonnie and Harriet exchanged glances.

Harriet said, "It's hell."

"It's worse than hell," Lonnie said. "They take an entire day to bore you to death."

"Then I won't do it."

They both looked shocked. "You have to," said Harriet, "otherwise the violation's on your record."

"Is that so bad?"

"You have no idea," said Lonnie. "For one thing, your insurance goes sky-high. Believe me, traffic school, painful though it will be, is the only way to go."

"Traffic school?" Ariana was standing in the doorway, looking so cool and contained I imagined the air around her must be a degree or so colder than the rest of the room.

Time for humble pie. "You were absolutely right, Ariana. I shouldn't have taken Dad's car. I've come a gutzer."

A shadow of alarm crossed her face. "And a gutzer would be?"

"No worries, the Mustang's all right. What I mean is, I was really a mug lair this morning, sailing along thinking I had everything under control. But when I came off the freeway I got confused and drove on the wrong side. Not for long, but long enough for a cop to see me and lower the boom."

"I see."

"I should be thrashed within an inch of my life," I declared.

The corners of Ariana's mouth curled. "I think traffic school will be punishment enough."

"It's *that* bad?"

She actually smiled. "Worse than you can imagine."

⊃

I wasn't keen on moving to the Deers' mansion this weekend. The reason I gave Ariana was I didn't want to leave poor Jules alone in the place all Sunday, just when she'd got used to having me around. Ariana may have guessed it was also because I was feeling rather more at home here at the office and didn't want to leave it.

There was something else too. I didn't trust Dave Deer. On the mansion's front steps, when we'd all been saying our farewells the night before, his hand had lingered on my shoulder, and his smile had seemed tinged with a hidden meaning. Perhaps it was my imagination, but I didn't think so. Back at the pub I'd had to beat off enough passes from blokes who'd hit the booze too hard not to recognize a come-on when I saw it. I'd take a bit of time and work out my strategy before I jumped feet-first into trouble.

Ariana gave Harriet time off to take me shopping to buy something new for the party tonight. I'd been resigned to wearing my plum dress again, so this was a bit of a surprise.

I got my second surprise—not nearly as welcome—when we got back a couple of hours later. A leggy, cheerful woman was waiting for Harriet. "Hi, honey," she said, followed by a kiss and a hug. Then she smiled widely at me. "I'm Beth. You must be Kylie. Harriet's told me all about you."

Major disappointment. It seemed I could cross Harriet Porter off my wish list.

My mind was taken off this setback by the arrival of Dr. Deer's security chief to discuss my undercover role.

We met in Ariana's office. "Fred Mills," he said, extending one pudgy hand. He had one of those clammy, spongy handshakes that always make me want to wipe my fingers afterward.

Ariana, I noticed, avoided shaking hands at all by retreating behind her desk.

"I've been liaising with Fred over the missing disks," she said to me, "so he's fully in the loop."

Frankly, looking at the piggy eyes and loose mouth of the security chief, I had my doubts this was a good thing. Fred Mills was middle-aged and not wearing it well. He had a gut that threatened to pop the buttons off his shirt and a thick neck bulging over his collar. And I'd describe his expression as a smirk shading into an outright leer.

Hands on hips, he stood back to look me up and down. "Well, well, and this is the undercover babe, eh?"

I glanced over at Ariana. She disguised it well, but I caught a look of distaste before her face became professionally blank again.

"Jeez, Fred," I said, "haven't been called a babe since I was in nappies."

"Nappies?"

"Diapers," Ariana translated.

"Heh, heh." Fred apparently thought I'd made a joke of some sort. When no one joined in, he stuck out his lower lip, and said in a truculent tone, "No need to get on your high horse. I was just being friendly."

"That's bonzer, Fred. Thank you so much. And how are you?"

He blinked at my cheery tone. "Me? I'm all right."

"Good-oh," I said. "So let's get down to business. Who do you think took the disks?"

Fred narrowed his piggy eyes until they almost disappeared in folds of flesh. "I believe that's Kendall & Creeling's worry, not mine. I'm concerned with the security of Dr. Deer's professional building in Beverly Hills and, of course, his home."

"Aren't patient records part of what you're supposed to secure?"

His jowls jiggled as he shook his head. "No, no. That's medical. I don't touch medical."

Ariana said, "The in-depth background checks on Deerdoc staff we've been doing are turning up some anomalies. It's apparent that some people would not have been offered jobs if the information had been available."

We got the jowl ripple again as he shook his head some more. "Not my responsibility. That's human resources."

"What is your responsibility, Fred?" I asked with genuine curiosity.

He shot me a look that said *Bitch!* but his words were mild. "I'm in charge of all measures to keep Dr. Deer and his wife safe and free from harassment. That includes maintaining the integrity of the two buildings, and in the case of his home the surrounding grounds as well."

He seemed pleased with his answer, which had the sound of something rehearsed.

I should have resisted asking, but I didn't. "Isn't the theft of the files breaking the integrity of the building, even if the files themselves aren't your responsibility?"

Fred gave an irritated grunt. "Look, little lady, I'm a professional. Ariana here's a professional too. If you don't mind me saying so, you're an amateur. A rank amateur. I don't want to be unkind, but to be brutal, you don't know what you're talking about. And if it was up to me, you wouldn't be in the picture at all."

Ariana dispatched a warning glance in my direction, which I took to mean she wanted me to stop chiaking this bloke. So I did, listening with hardly a comment while he rabbited on about how I had to report to him if I noticed anything unusual or noteworthy.

When he stood to go, his good humor had been restored. With a superior smile, he said, "Could be you'll get out of your depth. Could be you actually find something useful. Whatever, just holler, little lady, and I'll be there. Just holler."

Ariana saw him out and came back amused. "Reassured?" she said with a sardonic lift of an eyebrow.

"Heaps. This little lady just has to holler. Simple, really."

EIGHT

Ariana couldn't be seen giving me a lift to the Deers' function, and I wasn't game to drive the Mustang at night, so Fred Mills was to pick me up. He arrived in a shiny, bulky black vehicle that looked as though a truck and an SUV had mated. The cabin had four doors, and then there was a short truck bed tacked on behind it. Neither fish nor fowl, my mum would say.

With some difficulty I clambered into the front passenger seat. Thanks to the tightness of the lime-green dress Harriet had persuaded me to buy, I exposed more leg for Fred's inspection than intended. I swear I heard him smack his lips, and I had to fight not to deliver a smack of my own. The bloke was a major lech, and sooner or later I reckoned I'd have it out with him.

Thinking I might as well use the time with Fred to learn something useful, on the way I asked him questions about Deerdoc. He was delighted to be the expert, telling me more than he should about Dave Deer and his famous patients. Fred Mills had a loose mouth in more ways than one.

When we got to our destination the gates were open, manned by two burly guards with clipboards who checked us out then waved us through. Ignoring the fact that cars were queuing up behind us, Fred braked when he drew level with them. I figure he wanted to show off a bit. "Everything in order, men?"

"Yeah."

Fred's face darkened. "You mean, 'Yes, Mr. Mills.'"

"Yes, Mr. Mills." The guard's tone was insolent, but Fred didn't seem to notice.

We followed a stream of cars toward the house. "If you want to learn the inside story about security," Fred said, "you'll want to stick with me." His right hand hovered, as if he were going to pat my thigh. Lucky for him, he chickened out at the last moment.

Yerks! Fred's company on the drive over had been enough. Even if I had to hitch, I was getting back to Kendall & Creeling some other way.

The driveway near the house was lined with parked vehicles, lots of them bulky SUVs. When we got near the front door, there was a mini traffic jam. A couple of young men in black outfits were dashing around opening doors of arriving cars to let the passengers out, then leaping into the vehicles to drive them out of the way. Past the entrance was a bunch of big, black limousines lined up like beached whales. Drivers leaned against them, talking.

The house was lit up, just like last night, but this time there was noise. A buzz of conversation and music rose above the building like an invisible cloud. People were wandering everywhere. "Security must be a nightmare," I said to Fred, "seeing there's so many guests."

He took this as a criticism. "I've got a handle on it. Don't you worry, missy!"

It was a relief when we got to the head of the line and my door was opened. "See you later," I said to Fred, thinking no time was too soon.

"Now, wait a minute—"

I left him struggling to get his ungainly body out from behind the steering wheel.

The entrance was crowded with people all talking at the top of their voices. Just inside, the Deers were doing the greeting routine, smiles flashing on and off like dental semaphore. They seemed to have it down to a fine art, exclaiming with delight, warmly shaking hands, hugging, air-kissing, and generally giving incoming guests the big welcome.

When it was my turn, Elise, looking terrific in red, cried, "Kylie, at last!" before her attention was taken by the next guest.

Dave Deer took the opportunity to embrace me rather too closely. I smelled expensive aftershave and the Scotch he'd recently consumed. From working in a pub, I knew my liquor. If he kept breathing on me like this, I'd be able to identify the brand.

Trying not to be too obvious, I wriggled my way free. "My wife's cousin," he announced in a loud, ringing voice to anyone who cared to listen. It sounded so stagy I cringed. Whatever Dave Deer's talents might be, acting wasn't one of them.

A slight, older woman, with a face and bearing reminding me of pictures I'd seen of Nancy Reagan, said, "You're an Australian too, my dear?"

"Too right."

I was about to say more, but a bloke in a dark suit with a hearing-aid thing in his ear shepherded her away. Secret Service? I gazed after the two of them, fascinated. Maybe it *was* Nancy Reagan.

Crikey, and over there I'd bet a motza I was seeing Michael Douglas and Catherine Zeta-Jones chatting with Julie Andrews. Or maybe they were star look-alikes...

My gaze settled on someone who was doing a good imitation of being Brad Pitt. And was that shortish bloke Tom Cruise?

No one was listening to the string quartet playing classical music. Waiters circulated with trays of drinks and plates of bities. I snaffled a glass of champagne from one passing by, noticing he was smoothly handsome in a tanned, regular-featured sort of way. He flashed a quick electric smile when I thanked him. Now that I looked around, all the waiters, male and female, appeared to be good-looking.

Positioning myself beside double decorative columns—the architect of this place had column-mania, that much was clear—I settled down to enjoy eye-surfing the guests to see how many I could identify.

The columns formed a sort of little alcove, which turned out to be the perfect place to inadvertently eavesdrop. Like eddies in an ocean, people constantly moved around, often halting briefly near me. Bart Toller, one of the patients who'd had his disks stolen, was one. I recognized him immediately, as he'd been getting lots of attention recently for his scene-stealing supporting role in a movie based on Sigmund Freud's theories, a comedy called *The Id and I.*

Toller was alone, looking handsome but very down in the mouth. I was actually considering going over to him to say g'day and cheer him up when a man and woman approached, both bouncing along like the power couple I supposed they were.

"Bart!" he exclaimed.

"Gavin. Judy. Good to see you." I noted his enthusiasm factor was low.

"And great to see you, Bart," Gavin said warmly, pumping Toller's hand while simultaneously slapping him on the shoulder. "It's been too long. How's Kathy and the kids?"

Bart Toller's forced smile disappeared. "We're separated. Getting a divorce."

"Oh, man!" Another hearty whack to the shoulder. "I can't tell you how sorry I am to hear that."

Bart Toller excused himself and moved away. Gavin turned to Judy. "It's a mystery to me why she's stuck with Toller this long. He's such an asshole."

"At the salon yesterday I heard Kathy's hot and heavy with her personal trainer. Dumb as a post, but quite a performer between the sheets. Can hardly blame her. Bart's supposed to swing both ways..."

I was relieved when the couple drifted off. I hate that sort of goss, when someone else's genuine misery provides entertainment.

"Lime-green suits you," said a cool voice. I'd been so busy celebrity-spotting, I hadn't noticed Ariana approach. She saluted me with her champagne glass. Her pants and tunic top were black, of course, but embroidered with an elaborate gold and red design. Her pale blond hair was down. Her blue eyes glowed. She looked sensational.

"Do you always wear black?"

She took a sip of her drink, looking at me over the rim of the glass. "Not always. But usually."

Suddenly I had the thought that Ariana might be in mourning for someone and that was why she dressed in black. Maybe she'd been multicolored in the past, prior to the tragedy. "I shouldn't ask questions like that, Ariana. Sorry."

There was an awkward silence between us. I searched for some topic to fill it. "All the waiters are good-looking," I said. "Have you noticed that?"

"Most are actors, hoping to be discovered. Parties like this let them rub shoulders with the movers and shakers."

"Does anyone strike it lucky?"

Ariana shrugged. "Probably not the way they hoped."

A loud shout of laughter billowed from a large group near us. "Who's that?" I said, indicating a bloke who was tubby and toad-faced but wearing a suit that even I could see had to be very expensive. He stabbed the air with a huge cigar as he spoke in a penetrating, nasal voice to a captivated audience.

"Harvey Colby. A producer. Very big in the film business."

A skinny blond came gliding up to attach herself to Colby's

free arm. She fixed her wide-eyed stare on him with apparent adoration. She looked half his age and a quarter his weight.

Seeing me watching the woman, Ariana said, "Trophy wife number four, I believe. Or it could be five."

A perceptible rise in the hum of conversation indicated something was happening. "It's Jarrod Perkins," someone said in a reverent tone.

The Aussie director was making his way across the room, an entourage following in his wake. He hadn't gone to a lot of trouble dressing for the function. His blue jeans were faded, and he wore a black T-shirt under a shabby tweed jacket.

"Behold the artist," said Ariana sardonically.

The crowd parted before Perkins as though he deserved special attention. People called out greetings, flashed smiles, but nothing slowed his progress until he abruptly halted near us. He shoved his hands into the pockets of his jacket and snapped his head around, frowning petulantly.

This was the first time I'd seen him in the flesh, and all those unflattering photos turned out to be true. He was weedy, stoop-shouldered, and pigeon-toed. His thinning dark hair had been carefully combed over his scalp, but the pink showed through. His most notable feature was his nose, an enormous, curved beak that made him look like a ferocious parrot.

"Where's the fucking bar?" he half-shouted. "I need a fucking drink." A waiter tried to offer him champagne, but Perkins snarled, "A real drink, not lolly water." He jerked his head at the nearest in his support group. "Get me a bourbon on the rocks. Make it a triple. And don't fart around doing it."

Astonishingly, there was a ripple of appreciative laughter at his rudeness.

"Jeez," I whispered to Ariana, "if he's that bad-tempered, he must have heard about the disks."

"This is Jarrod Perkins on a good day," she said with scorn. "You should see him when things go wrong."

"Beats me why anyone puts up with him."

"He can get away with anything because he's a successful director. That makes him a god in this town."

A delicious picture of Jarrod Perkins in therapy popped into my mind. I visualized Dave Deer taking personal pleasure in delivering the blows in Slap! Slap! Get On With It to this particular patient.

Ariana gave me a gentle shove. "You shouldn't be seen talking to me for more than a few casual minutes. Circulate, Kylie. Get to know some people. That's what Elise's cousin would do."

Five minutes later, as I was obediently mingling, Elise herself found me. "Kylie, dear. There are some people you *must* meet!"

Soon I was dizzy with introductions to individuals whose names I wouldn't remember and who weren't at all interested in me. Then Elise swept me into the larger dining room, which was absolutely huge and filled with people screaming "Darling!" and laughing extravagantly at one another's jokes. Mounds—no, mountains—of food were arranged on tables lining the walls. White-aproned waiters rushed around serving guests too lazy or busy to serve themselves. There was even a meat station, where a bloke with a wicked carving knife cut slices from various roasted meats.

So I ate, and chatted, and tried to smile like everyone else. I was getting jack of the nonstop noise and endless parade of faces, though, and longed to escape. But how?

"And when are you moving in with us, Kylie?" said Dave Deer in my ear. "Tomorrow?" He attempted to put an arm around my waist, but I nimbly moved. Plainly he'd been chug-a-lugging the scotch all night.

"Perhaps next week. I'll let you know."

He squeezed my arm. "I look forward to it."

"Lovely party," I said. "Thank you so much."

"You're not leaving?" He looked quite put-out. "The night is young, as they say."

Groan. "I'm still a bit jet-lagged," I said. Of course I wasn't, and he probably knew it, but he nodded obligingly. "Would you thank Elise for me?" He wrinkled his brow. "Your wife," I added helpfully.

At this point someone claimed Dave's attention, so I took the op to get away. Ariana. I had to find her. A horrible thought struck—perhaps she'd already left. If so, I could throw myself on Fred's mercy. Or I could just slash my wrists right now.

I found her talking with a pleasantly ordinary man whose best characteristic, at least in these surroundings, was his low-key manner. He ducked his head almost shyly as Ariana introduced him.

"Kylie, this is Dr. Vincent Adams. He's at Deerdoc, and he's aware you'll be working there next week."

Dr. Adams gave me a moderate smile, a relief after all the teeth I'd seen exposed tonight. "Call me Vince," he said in a quiet, gentle tone.

We all made light conversation for a few minutes, then he was called away by an imperious command from an old woman wearing enough bright jewelry to decorate a Chrissie tree.

"I want to go home," I said to Ariana. "Any chance of a lift? I can't face Fred again."

"Sure. Do you want to go now?"

"Blood oath, I do."

"I'll say my farewells and meet you outside. Go down the drive a little way, so I can pick you up without anyone seeing."

The night was cool and mercifully quiet. I threw my head back to check out the stars but could only see a few of the brighter ones. Back in the 'Gudge, even on moonless nights, if there were no clouds, the Milky Way arching across the sky provided starlight enough to see your way.

"Ready to go home, little lady?" said a voice close behind me. "I'm at your service."

Fred Mills. I turned around fast, nearly taking off his nose. "I've got a lift home, thanks."

Not pleased, Fred said, "Don't you know the good old American custom that says you go home with the boy who brought you?"

"No worries. Ariana's leaving now, and I asked her to drop me off."

With relief I saw Ariana emerge from the building. I'd run the chance of someone seeing us together. "Over here," I shrieked.

She nodded to Fred. "Evening." To me she said, "Ready?"

"You've no idea how much."

When Ariana retrieved her car and we were leaving, I looked back. Fred Mills was standing splay-legged, his arms folded over this corpulent chest.

I'd made an enemy. My first in L.A.

NINE

Sunday was a gorgeous day. I had my breakfast with Julia Roberts in dappled sunshine out in the backyard under the citrus trees. I'd wedged the back door so it couldn't spring closed and lock, dragged out a box from the storeroom to use as a table and a spare chair from the nearest office. Perhaps I could persuade Ariana to fund a garden table and chairs. I tut-tutted to myself. Here I was forgetting half the place was mine. I could simply instruct Fran to get the furniture and it would be done. Or not. Fran was still an unknown quantity. I had no idea at what point she would buck an order, but I didn't doubt there was such a point.

Jules had plunked her tawny self in a large patch of sunshine, opening her green eyes now and then to check if potential prey had materialized. I realized what a poor excuse for a hunter she was when an inquisitive bird hopped onto a low branch to eyeball her. Julia lashed her tail a bit then lost interest, gave a wide pink yawn, and dozed off again.

I'd never seen a squirrel in real life before but recognized what the little thing was when it leapt from the roof onto one of the trees and ran headfirst down the trunk, where it stopped, fluffy tail vibrating, upside down. I thought Julia Roberts would jump up and clobber the intruder, or at the very least look dangerous, but she regarded it without interest, and shut her eyes again.

"Call yourself a cat," I hooted. "Any Aussie feline would be up and at that squirrel."

My heart did a gymnastic leap when a voice said, "Julia Roberts is incurably lazy." It was the beautiful, the spoken-for Harriet Porter.

"Crikey," I said, "you scared the living daylights out of me."

"Didn't Ariana call? She said she would."

"I wouldn't have heard the phone. Jules and I have been out here for ages."

She grinned at me. "And you're asking yourself what I'm doing here this Sunday morning, when I could be breakfasting in bed with Beth?"

This was altogether too intimate a picture, especially as I recalled breakfasts with Raylene that began with bacon and eggs and ended with something far more exciting.

"I'll bite," I said. "Why are you here?"

"Ariana called me this morning and asked if I cared to be paid double-time to help you rent a car, get a cell phone, and look at some clothes for your stint as Dr. Deer's assistant."

"Was it the pleasure of my company that persuaded you or the double time?"

"I won't lie to you," said Harriet. "I can be bought, I'm afraid. Money's tight this month, and it was an offer too good to refuse."

"Want a cuppa before we get started? I'll make a fresh pot."

"Tea? That'd be nice."

After finding another chair for Harriet and checking how she had her tea, I zipped into the kitchen, filled the electric jug, and switched it on. Tea-making was an art, and I followed to the letter the method Mum had taught me when I was a kid. First, half a cup of boiling water in the teapot to warm it for a few moments, then swirl it around and tip it out. Second, add one spoonful of tea for each person, plus one for the pot. Third, pour in boiling—repeat *boiling*—water that has to be actually bubbling. Finally, let steep for four minutes.

When I appeared with the mugs, Harriet was sprawled in a chair with her legs extended into direct sunlight. "What have you been doing? I was about to come in to look for you."

"Making tea."

"Oh, of course," said Harriet, light dawning. "You don't use tea bags, do you?"

"Not on your nelly!"

Harriet laughed. "What's a nelly?"

"You know, I've got no idea."

It was a lovely, peaceful morning. A butterfly or two flapped around, birds tweeted, Julie Roberts rolled on her back and waved her feet in the air. Harriet, positively glowing with health, sat with me in companionable silence.

I broke it by saying, "You look so terrific. Must be clean living."

"I think it's the fact that I'm pregnant."

"You are?"

My surprise made Harriet grin. "In case you're wondering, Kylie, a gay friend's the father, via a syringe. Genetically, Maurice is excellent. Just as important, Beth and I adore both him and his partner, Gary."

I felt a jab of envy. Harriet was someone who knew pretty well where her life was going and was clearly delighted with the direction it was taking. Plus she had a loving companion by her side for the journey, and dear friends to light the way...

I gave myself a hard mental slap. If I kept this up I'd soon be snuffling into my tea.

I asked, "Does Ariana know you're going to have a baby?"

"She insists on being godmother."

Cool, enigmatic Ariana as a godmother, cooing over a kicking infant? "You know Ariana well," I said, phrasing it as a statement, not a stickybeak question.

"As well as she lets anyone know her."

"A woman of mystery," I said lightly.

Harriet gave me an amused look. "Before you ask, I'm not altogether sure."

I felt myself beginning to blush. "Hell's bells, am I that obvious?"

"Uh-huh."

Now I was definitely red in the face. "I've been wondering since I met her if she's a lesbian. Dad never said one way or the other. With most people, you can pick up clues, but Ariana..." I shrugged.

"Beth and I have discussed it at length, believe me. Ariana never talks about her personal life. Beth thinks it's because she doesn't have one, that she's essentially sexless, rather like Lonnie. Neither of them seem particularly interested in relationships."

"I wouldn't compare Ariana to Lonnie," I said, indignant.

Harriet chuckled. "Only in that one respect are they alike. And who knows? Maybe Ariana has a scorching sex life we know nothing about." She looked at her watch. "We'd better get a move on—things to do and money to spend."

I collected a protesting Jules—Melodie had made it clear she wasn't allowed outside without supervision—and followed Harriet through the back door. Ariana with a scorching sex life? The idea didn't please me much. I had to admit I'd rather picture Ariana all alone, high up in her Hollywood Hills home, waiting for someone—well, waiting for *me*—to come bounding in and declare, "Let me take you to places you've never been before."

No, I'd have to rephrase. That sounded too much like a tourist agent. How about, "Together, we can make wonderful music"? No, that's worse. I should be more direct. I could say, "I lust after you, burn for you..." Nix that. Ariana would flatten me with her cold blue stare, or worse, laugh. Maybe I should let my actions speak louder than words and—

"Kylie? I don't want to hurry you, but we haven't got all day."

"Sorry."

I picked up my shoulder bag, resolutely banning further thoughts of Ariana Creeling. That way lay madness.

Harriet was nothing if not efficient. We hopped into her old Volvo and set out for the nearest shopping center. In short order I had a mobile phone and some really nice clothes to mix and match so I'd have several outfits for my undercover identity. Last was the rental car. Without probs I acquired a four-door, light-tan vehicle filled with the smell of artificial pine. It was a car without much character. Strewth, compared to Dad's Mustang, it didn't have *any* character. An automatic, it was no sweat to drive, but no fun either.

I thanked Harriet and said goodbye to her at the rental place. She was sweet and asked me if I wanted to join her and Beth for dinner, but I said I wanted an early night. Then I drove back to Kendall & Creeling. There was lots of traffic, and I seemed to snag every red light, so I stop-and-started the whole way, using the time to dwell on the fact Harriet hadn't been asked to help me find accommodation.

Last thing last night I'd said to Ariana, "I should get a flat somewhere near the office, don't you think?"

I would've thought she'd be pleased to get me out of the office bedroom suite, but she hadn't given the impression of jumping for joy. "You can look for an apartment when you have a better sense of L.A. and know where you'd prefer to be," she'd said.

"Melodie or Harriet can help," I'd said. "They know the whole area, don't they? I'd be happy to take advice."

"I don't think you should rush into a lease. If you sign one, you'll be committed to an apartment for at least a year."

I hadn't seen it last night, but now I realized Ariana didn't want me to put down roots. If I remained in the office bedroom, it was a temporary thing. I could go walkabout any time. It all boiled down to one fact: She didn't want me involved in the business. She was just biding her time until I caved and she bought me out.

She could bide all the time she liked. That wasn't going to happen. I was going to implement the Wombat Strategy. A wombat is unstoppable, once its mind is set on a goal. Just like that furry little tank, I'd set my course and I'd keep on keeping on.

When I thought about the drive home last night, I realized the freeze had really set in even before I'd mentioned getting a flat. Ariana, reassuringly sober, had been driving defensively, a wise decision since the roads appeared to be teeming with vehicles performing erratic maneuvers. I'd made a casual remark about wanting to look over Kendall & Creeling's books.

She'd glanced over at me with a frown. "You're free to discuss the financial situation with our accountants." Then she'd really got up my nose by adding, "I believe that would be best. Unless you're an expert, Kylie, financial records can be incomprehensible."

"Oh, I think I might muddle my way through," I said with heavy sarcasm. I'd looked after the financial side of Wombat's Retreat, and I figured a pub's books were going to be quite a lot more complicated than those of a private eye business.

I had no thought Ariana was cooking the books—I was sure she wasn't—but if my partnership with her was to work, I wanted to know every single thing about the company.

A chilly silence had fallen between us at this point. Looking for somewhere to live had struck me as a safe, neutral topic. Major miscalculation.

つ

I spent the rest of the day going to a Laundromat, usefully within walking distance from the offices, planning how I'd get out of moving into the Deers' mansion, and calling Mum to see how things were in the 'Gudge. It was late Sunday afternoon here and Monday morning there.

Not surprisingly, since it was less than a week since I'd skipped, nothing much had happened. With a certain wry satisfaction I learned that Mum's fiancé, Jack, was already having a bit of trouble mastering the finer points of running a pub.

Mum asked—hopefully, I thought—if I'd be coming home any time soon. I said although L.A. wasn't a patch on Wollegudgerie— Mum expected me to say that, so I did—I was finding it a very interesting place, so I'd stay a while. Mum asked if I'd seen any stars yet, and I filled her in with info on last night's party.

Without fail Mum has her hair done every Friday at 'Gudge's hairdressing salon, so I knew she would have seen Raylene's new love, Maria. I was burning to ask if she had any news of Raylene but with great effort managed not to bring up the subject.

With the unerring instinct of a mother, Mum said, "I ran into Raylene yesterday at the drycleaners. She asked after you."

I could see Raylene as clearly as if she were standing in front of me. She had beautifully silky hair that fell straight to her shoulders and a mobile, expressive face. I'd always loved her laugh, an infectious, bubbling sound.

"How is she?" I said, as if I didn't care one way or the other.

"She's fine. Said she was planning a trip to Bangkok during the next school break. She and Maria."

That was a stab to the heart. Raylene and I had talked at length about visiting Thailand. We'd pored over maps and brochures and plotted our itinerary. And now she was going there with Maria.

"Kylie, it's no good running away from your problems." Mum was in her I'm-saying-this-for-your-own-good mode. "Stand and face them, I always say."

"I'm not running away."

Mum clicked her tongue impatiently. "Of course you are. Just because a relationship doesn't work, it's no reason to shoot through."

"I don't want to talk about it."

"America's a dangerous place." Mum was getting het-up. "I see it on the telly every night. People getting shot for no reason at all. You're not safe there. I want you back here in Wollegudgerie."

Suddenly furious that she was ordering me around like I was a child, I said, "I'm not coming back. Not yet."

"When, then?" My mum was great at pinning people down. "Next month? For Chrissie? When?"

"Jeez, Mum, give it a rest."

Mum changed tack. "I really need you here, you know. Running the pub's no picnic without you. Jack's doing his best, but he hasn't learned the ropes yet."

"He will."

Silence. Then Mum said brightly, "Let's not fight, darling. You'll come home when you're ready. I know that."

We chatted about safe topics for a few minutes, then said goodbye. I put down the phone with the resigned feeling that she hadn't given up yet. She never does. Tenacity should be her middle name.

After that conversation I felt hungry, so I went for a walk to a Kentucky Fried Chicken place I'd noticed earlier. I bought extra, just in case Julia Roberts felt like a change from tinned cat food.

Jules and I ate chicken, watched TV, and generally lazed around. I reckoned I'd need all my energy for the week to come, so I aimed on having an early night. Every now and then during the evening, Jules did her startled staring routine, but I told her she could bung it on all she liked, I wasn't falling for it.

I was getting used to the noises of this place: the odd sounds that belonged to the house itself, of floors settling and beams expanding or contracting; the whine of urgent sirens in the distance; the muted, rumbling roar of traffic; the scatter of little feet on the tiles, which I devoutly hoped were squirrels, not rats; the trills and vocal embellishments of not one but now two mockingbirds, each set on attracting a mate.

"Jules," I said, "tomorrow is the first day of my new career as private investigator. What do you think of that?"

I thought she smiled, just a little.

TEN

"Fran, it was, like, love at first sight, you know what I mean?"
Melodie thumped herself on the chest with one clenched fist. I
expected her to cough, but she didn't. "Straight to the heart,
love's arrow hit me hard."

"Oh, yeah?" said Fran, leaning her slight form against the
kitchen bench, arms folded. Her red hair and translucent skin
made her seem like a painted porcelain doll with a D-cup bra
and a bleak expression.

"Isn't that a line from your last audition, Melodie?" Lonnie
sniggered. A glare from Melodie didn't quell him. He left the
kitchen with his mug of coffee saying, "Love's arrow hit me hard?
Oh, *please!*"

I stirred my porridge. "Is this someone new?"

"Oh, yes. Rich Westholme." She smiled reflectively. "Rich
Westholme. Isn't that a great name? We met on Saturday night
and hit it off right away." She paused, then said with deep signif-
icance, "He's a director."

"Never heard of him," said Fran. "What's he directed? A ten-
minute short in film school?"

Melodie was indignant. "Rich's *Ten Conversations With an
Angry Man* was shown at Sundance. And his latest movie, *Slow-
Slow Fast-Fast*, will be on that cable show about young directors

to watch out for. And Rich's got an A-list producer interested in his new project." She gave Fran a so-there glower.

"I've still never heard of him."

"Is he good-looking?" I asked, to deflect the coming explosion.

"*Intense* is how I'd describe Rich," said Melodie.

Fran sniffed. "That means no."

Ignoring this, Melodie said, "Rich and I spent all of Sunday together. It's just uncanny, the way we clicked. You know, I think he might be the *one*."

Fran raised a skeptical eyebrow. "He's offered you a part in one of his future masterpieces, hasn't he?"

Melodie tossed her head, causing her hair to fly around in an attractive arc. I'd bet quids she'd practiced that move in a mirror. "What if he has?"

"There's one born every minute," Fran said. "Every damn minute."

I looked over at Melodie and blinked. Her body language had abruptly changed to what I mentally labeled "extreme entreaty." "Fran," she said in a wheedling tone, "my agent called, and there's an audition—"

"No," said Fran. "Ask Lonnie."

"Lonnie says he can't. Oh, *please,* Fran. It's only for a couple of hours this afternoon."

"A couple of hours? I've heard that story before. Forget it. I'm not doing it."

Melodie turned her wide-eyed gaze on me. "Kylie? Could you help me out here?"

"Sorry, I'm due at Deerdoc this morning."

An airy wave of her hand indicated this was no prob. "But you're just meeting Dr. Deer's assistant to get an idea of what the job's about. You'll be back here by lunchtime."

"So it's true what you said."

"What?"

"Receptionists know everything that's going on."

Only slightly discomforted, Melodie admitted, "I did over-hear something..." Her grin grew cheeky. "So that means you can help me out."

I shook my head. "Sorry."

As I left the kitchen I heard Melodie say to Fran, "Is Harriet in yet...?"

⊃

Armed with driving instructions, I made it to Beverly Hills in good time, and on the correct side of the road the whole way. The Deerdoc building was on Roxbury Drive, and by good luck I found a parking meter nearby, fed it with coins, and bought myself a couple of hours before I'd score the attentions of the parking authorities.

I'd been sternly warned by, of all people, Fran, who gave me the good oil about Beverly Hills. Apparently it wasn't like other places in Los Angeles. For one thing, it had its own Beverly Hills cops, and they were fierce. "Don't talk back to them," Fran had said. "Pretend you're a tourist and you haven't got a clue." She laughed unkindly at that point. "Which would be true, because you haven't."

She'd advised me the parking officers were even more vicious than the cops, but had reserved her harshest comments for the matrons of Beverly Hills. "Run you down as soon as look at you," she declared. "Dressed to the nines and totally ruthless."

So far unscathed, I approached the Deerdoc Enterprises building, stopping on the way to give the once-over to a huge, lumbering vehicle I'd seen in advertised a zillion times on teev last night. It beat me how anyone could park one of these

Hummers, let alone drive it without sideswiping cars in the adjacent lane.

The Deerdoc building had three stories and a graceful facade. A doorman in a dark-blue uniform allowed me to enter the mirrored lobby, which was dominated by a huge display of flowers in an alabaster vase. A second man in a similar well-tailored uniform stepped forward to check my credentials, murmured into a phone, then directed me to a thickly carpeted lift.

The doors shut with a well-mannered sigh. The walls here were mirrored too. I imagined many of Dave Deer's patients spent a good part of their lives fighting time's consequences with exercise, diets, and plastic surgery, so constant inspections in mirrors would be automatic. Not to be left out, I checked myself over. Dark hair: short, shiny. Face: the minimum makeup of powder and lipstick. Clothes: a plain, tailored blue dress. Jewelry: a watch and stud opal earrings.

The lift hissed open. DAVID DEER read the black lettering on the highly polished blue door facing me. Inside, someone had gone overboard with an Australian theme. The plush carpeting was the color of red earth; distinctive Aboriginal dot paintings were displayed on ocher walls; a didgeridoo at least two meters long was mounted on a stand; boomerangs somersaulted across a partition separating an alcove from the rest of the room.

There were two fish tanks, each dominating an entire wall. One was full of brightly colored fish. Tiny iridescent ones darted in little packs as larger, garish specimens swam lazily through columns of bubbles. A sign indicated these tropical fish were all natives of the Great Barrier Reef.

The second tank featured sharks, each small but deadly looking. They cruised with graceful menace.

"How may I help you?" The woman behind the rough-hewn

slab that served as a desk had smooth dark skin, an elegant neck, and a pouting red mouth. A nameplate revealed her name to be Chantelle.

Someone coughed, and I realized there was a person in the alcove behind the screen.

"G'day. I'm Kylie Kendall. I'm here to see Noreen."

"Of course. You're Noreen's replacement while she's on vacation."

"That's about it," I said. "I'm here to get an idea of how things run." I directed a warm smile at her. "I've heard tell receptionists know everything that's going on in any business, so I reckon you'd be my go-to person."

Chantelle looked gratified. "It's true," she said in a near whisper, "but you'd be the first I've met who realizes it."

There was renewed coughing behind the screen, then the sound of a match flaring, followed by the unmistakable sigh as a smoker exhaled the first stream of smoke.

Chantelle's expression blended irritation and resignation. She clicked her tongue. "There's no smoking allowed in the building. State law." Even so, she made no move to rebuke the smoker.

"A celebrity?" I said, looking toward the dividing screen.

Chantelle's red lips formed themselves into a disapproving line. "Minor only. Major celebrities have their own private entrance."

"And the waiting room?" I indicated the row of chairs awaiting patients.

"Nonentities," she said, "but with money."

She pressed a button set into the surface of the polished slab. "I'll get Noreen to show you around."

After a moment a door, set so well into the wall behind Chantelle it was invisible, suddenly opened. A glossy blond wearing a tight pink dress and very high-heeled sandals appeared, smiling. "Kylie? Come this way." She had a soft, breathy, confiding voice. "I'm Noreen, Dr. Deer's personal assistant."

She took my arm. She only came up to my shoulder, even with her heels. She had blue eyes, a pale version of Ariana's. Her blond hair cascaded in curls down her back.

I said, "Fair dinkum, no offense, but there's an awful lot of blonds in L.A."

"Blonds have more fun," Noreen said, as though no one had ever said this before.

"That explains it, then."

She took me down a corridor, lushly carpeted. All I could hear was the faint hiss of air conditioning. "Every room is sound-proofed," she said, "so primal screams cannot disturb other patients."

"Right-oh."

She patted my arm as though we'd been mates for yonks. "I'd show you Dr. Deer's room, but he has a patient with him at the moment."

"Where the fucking hell is Dave Bloody Deer?"

"Aw, shit!" said Noreen under her breath.

Jarrod Perkins, head lowered aggressively, had entered the hall behind us. He was dressed in the same clothes—jeans, T-shirt, and tweed jacket—he'd worn Saturday night.

"I've got a fucking bloody appointment," he snarled. "Where is the son of a bitch, eh?"

Hands fluttering, Noreen tottered on her high heels toward him. "Dr. Deer will be with you in a moment, Mr. Perkins. He wants you to know he has a medical emergency."

"Fuck that for a joke!" Perkins began striding toward us, his arms windmilling. "Get out of my way."

A man I recognized as the doorman materialized. "Anyone here own a Hummer? Yellow one? Parked in the handicapped zone in front of the building?"

Jarrod Perkins swung around. "That's mine. Forget about a bloody parking ticket. I never pay them anyway."

"It's not a parking ticket, sir."

"What then? The fucking bastards aren't trying to tow the fucking thing away, are they?"

"No, sir. Perhaps you'd like to come down. The police are here."

"What are the fucking police here for?"

"It's the Hummer, sir." He paused, and I swear I saw a smile flicker on his lips. "There appears to have been a bomb. Your Hummer's blown up. Completely destroyed."

ELEVEN

Jarrod Perkins's misfortune spread through the office like wildfire. Noreen hurried off to find Dave Deer and give him the news, and I joined the mini-rush hastening downstairs to see the exploded Hummer.

Chantelle was on the phone. As I passed her desk I heard her say, "KNX? Have I got a hot news tip for you!"

Outside, quite a few people had already gathered to gaze at the wreck. Fred Mills was on the scene, running around like a chook with its head chopped off, his horrified gaze fixed on the smoking remains of the hulking Hummer. "Happened in a public place," he mumbled. "Not my responsibility. Not my responsibility at all."

Jarrod Perkins was standing by what was left of his vehicle, turning the air blue. One young cop was deadset to shut him up, but I saw an older one say something to him, and he backed off.

I could imagine Ariana saying dryly, "The privileges of celebrity status."

It was quite a scene: Perkins frothing at the mouth, a bunch of cops glaring around as if any minute now the guilty party would spring out of the rapidly collecting crowd and confess, fire engines arriving with sirens screaming. Overhead helicopters were buzzing like blowies scenting dead meat.

And there was the indescribable smell of burnt Hummer. The

vehicle was a crumpled, once-yellow shell, its fat tires melted into the roadway. Vehicles parked behind and in front had sustained considerable damage. Broken glass littered the area, and across the road a car alarm had been set off by the blast and was he-hawing fit to bust.

I was having a gander when Dave Deer grabbed my arm, saying urgently, "Kylie, you've got a car?"

I pointed. "Down the street."

His fingers tightened until I gave a yelp. "The exit to our parking garage is blocked. I'm relying on you to get Perkins out of here before the media trucks arrive."

"He won't come with me. Take a look at him."

Hard to believe the bloke hadn't run out of steam: He was still spewing curses at the top of his voice.

"I'll handle Perkins. Start your car and get ready to get him out of here."

Dave Deer was as good as his word. Two minutes later he was bundling Perkins into the passenger seat.

"How'd you do that?" I asked, amazed. The director had even shut up.

"Half price on all future therapy." He looked up as a network TV truck roared up, closely followed by a second media vehicle. Cameras, reporters, and support staff spilled out at a run.

Deer slapped the roof of my car. "Get going!"

I set off sedately, even signaled that I was pulling out, not that anyone was looking. Everyone was hurrying to view the corpse of the Hummer, probably hoping there were other corpses too. Everyone except a lone parking cop, who was methodically writing tickets. I had the bizarre thought that when she worked her way up the row she'd give a ticket to the wrecked Hummer for being blown up while parked illegally in a handicapped zone.

"Where do you want to go?" I asked Perkins.

His head was sunk into his puny shoulders, and he was glaring out the windscreen. "Take me home."

"I don't know where home is."

He swung around to look at me for the first time. This close up, the bloke was even less appealing. His gigantic nose made his eyes seem like small black dots placed there as an afterthought. "Who are you?"

"G'day. I'm Kylie Kendall."

"Not your name," he snapped. "Who are you?"

"Dr. Deer's personal assistant. Temporary only."

He grunted, fished in his pocket and took out a mobile phone. Punching in a number, he listened with growing impatience. "Ah, Jesus Christ! Pick up, you bastard."

"If you don't tell me where to go," I said, "I'll drive in circles till you do."

"What?"

"You've got to direct me, Mr. Perkins. I have no idea where your house is."

"Hollywood Hills."

I had a vague idea of the general location, off to the north of Sunset. Ariana lived there. Maybe she and Perkins were neighbors. But wouldn't she have said so before? Perhaps not. Ariana wasn't noted for blabbing personal information.

Perkins had given up on that particular call and was punching another number. "Jill? The fucking Hummer's a total write-off..."

While he continued with his expletive-laced conversation— seemingly to someone in P.R.—I wondered about the possibility that the explosion was somehow linked to the blackmail threat. But why not just ask for money? Why run the risk of planting a bomb? If it was to intimidate, Jarrod Perkins wouldn't make the connection, because he hadn't been told about the missing therapy disks. Of course, maybe the blackmailer didn't realize this.

"Turn left here! Watch out for the fucking bus." When I'd darted through a gap in the traffic and completed the left turn more or less successfully, Perkins went back to his phone. He finished one call and began another. "Sven? Open the gates. I'm five minutes away...I'm on the tube? What are they saying about me? Mention my latest movie? ...Yes, of course I'm fucking well all right."

Once we were off the main arteries, the way narrowed so much it seemed there would hardly be room for two cars to pass. The road rose steeply, winding in hairpin bends between houses built right up to the edge. I couldn't imagine how Perkins could negotiate this route in something as wide as a Hummer.

"Turn right! Jesus! This next street!"

Tires squealing, I made the turn. "I'd appreciate it if you gave me more warning."

Astonishingly, a faint smile appeared on his face. "You'd appreciate it, would you? I must try to do better."

I rolled my eyes at his sarcasm, then whipped the wheel around when he screamed, "Turn right! Now left! Take the driveway on your right."

The gates were open. Apparently Sven, whoever he was, had come through. The drive wound its way ever upward, until we crested the rise and came to a flat parking area. The house perched on the brink of the cliff, hanging on for dear life so it wouldn't slide over. It was an ungainly building, with a roof that looked like a big flat cap pulled down to shade its glass walls.

The view, however, was a bit of all right. My mum would have said it was more a vista, or maybe a panorama. Even with smog blurring the outlines of the tall buildings, I could see a spectacular view of downtown Los Angeles. At night the lights of the city spread out like a blanket would be worth a second look.

A bulky, crew-cut, blond bloke, with thigh muscles so over-developed he was forced to waddle, came out of the house and opened the passenger door. Jarrod Perkins got out. "Did you contact my attorney? Someone's responsible. I'll sue the pants off them, the bastards."

If I'd been holding out for thanks, or even an acknowledgment I'd gone out of my way to chauffeur him here, I would have been one disappointed dame. But I wasn't, and he didn't. Without one word to me, he left Sven holding the door, turned his back on us both, and stalked into the house.

Sven closed the door. I waited until he was my side of the car. Giving him a little farewell wave, I said, "And the pity of it is, I didn't even get an autograph."

He smirked. I drove off.

A few wrong turns later, I was on Hollywood Boulevard. I'd been studying the Thomas Guide, and thought I knew exactly where I was. My confidence was misplaced. Shortly I found myself heading in quite the wrong direction on a street I didn't recognize—which didn't mean much, since I didn't recognize most of them.

Being lost turned out to be a good thing, though, because I noticed a huge bookstore and turned into its parking lot with only a couple of near-collisions on the way. Inside I found the information desk, manned by a pimply boy with the first bad teeth I'd noticed since I hit L.A. "Help you?" he asked without much interest. He brightened up at my reply.

"I'm thinking of becoming a private eye," I said. "Is there a book you'd recommend?"

"A private eye?" he sounded almost enthusiastic. "Come right this way."

⊃

As soon as I entered the reception area, Melodie latched onto me. "You've got to tell me every detail! Was Jarrod Perkins real upset? Did you see inside his house?"

"Crikey," I said. "How do you know I drove him home? Receptionist hotline?"

"Chantelle called and clued me in. And she said you were real nice to her."

An incoming call interrupted. "Hold, please. I'll see if she's available." Melodie made a face at me. "It's Fran's husband," she confided, "and I just know she won't want to talk to him."

Fran was *married*! I contemplated what it must be like living with her thundercloud face. You wouldn't want to be a depressive or you'd slit your throat.

Apparently Fran did want to talk to him, so Melodie put the call through, then got back to business. "Did you hear the bang?"

"The whole place is soundproof, so you can't hear a thing. First anyone knew was when the doorman turned up to give Jarrod Perkins the bad news."

"You didn't hear the explosion?" Melodie was clearly disappointed in me.

I shook my head. "No explosion, but I was standing next to Jarrod Perkins when he learned his Hummer had blown up."

"No!" exclaimed Melodie, delighted. "Like, how did he take it?"

I visualized the director's bulging eyes and contorted face. "Not too well."

"They're saying it's a terrorist attack. It's on all the networks. Chantelle says the whole of Deerdoc is in an uproar. And when Dr. Deer called a few minutes ago, he sounded real shook up, know what I mean?"

"I'd better report to Ariana."

Before I'd left the reception area, Melodie was on the phone. "Tiffany? Oh, my God! You'll never guess what's happened..."

Ariana's unruffled persona was soothing, after the excitement I'd just been through. "Wouldn't it rot your socks?" I said, slumping into a chair. "No sooner do I get to Deerdoc, all keen to learn the ropes, when bam! A bomb goes off. It was a bomb, wasn't it?"

"Nothing's confirmed. I'll call a friend on the bomb squad later this afternoon and find out what they know."

"It could have been a fuel leak, or some electrical short."

"Could be, but there's no doubt Perkins has a knack for making enemies."

I slipped off my shoes and wriggled my feet. I couldn't imagine tottering around on really high heels all day, but maybe it was a matter of practice, like ballerinas standing on their toes.

Ariana said, "Dave Deer's just called. You're starting work at Deerdoc tomorrow. Nine sharp."

"Fair go, Noreen hasn't taken me through her duties yet. I wouldn't know what to do."

"It's your opportunity to be creative. Noreen's put in her resignation as of this afternoon. She says she's not going to be a victim of international terrorism."

I had a little smile at that, trying to come up with a scenario that'd have international terrorists blowing up an Aussie director's Hummer in Beverly Hills.

"Don't see how it's terrorism," I said, "unless Perkins is leading a double life as a spy."

"The attack's more likely to be tied to the theft of the therapy disks. If so, it's imperative you find who in the Deerdoc organization took them."

"Isn't 'imperative' a nice word?" I said. "Makes things sound important."

"It *is* important, Kylie."

Ariana hardly ever used my name, and I was caught unaware when I got a little thrill when she did.

"I've just found out Fran's married." A total change of subject

111

would get my mind off the thrill before it developed into something more.

Ariana sat back in her chair and gave me her patented long, blue stare.

"You do a lot of that," I said.

"A lot of what?"

"Sitting back and giving me the hairy eyeball, like you really don't approve."

Ariana threw back her head and laughed, really laughed.

"What's funny?" I said, not joining in.

Still smiling, she shook her head. "I don't think I can put it into words."

"You could try."

Her face sobered, until she was her usual detached self. "We need to discuss your undercover role in detail. I'll bring Bob in on it too. He's an expert in this sort of thing. I'm booked for the rest of the day. Are you free for dinner?"

"Julia Roberts will be disappointed, but I think I can make it."

"Good. I'll speak to Bob and get back to you."

I beat a dignified retreat from her office. Okay, I'd managed to make her laugh at me. Laughing *with* me was next on the agenda.

When I went to the kitchen in search of a cuppa, I found Bob Verritt had been cornered by Melodie, who hovered at the door with one ear cocked to catch the phone in reception. Lonnie, grinning, provided an audience.

"Bob," she was saying, "this audition's super important for my career, or I wouldn't ask."

Bob, so much taller than all of us, had his narrow shoulders hunched and was sort of bent over, like a big question mark. "Look at it from my point of view, Melodie. I can't be in front and answer the phone. I've got too much work to do."

"I could switch it so every call rang through to your office..." She batted her eyelashes at him.

"I don't think so." He grinned at me. "Help me here, Kylie. This woman's implacable."

The implacable woman wasn't giving up. "I just can't miss this audition! Did you read *The Hollywood Reporter* this morning? It says the network's likely to pick up the show for an entire season. My agent says I've got a real good chance of getting the angel sidekick."

"Something like *Charlie's Angels*?" said Bob.

"No, the sort with feathers. The heavenly ones."

Lonnie said, "Angel shows are *so* yesterday."

"Not *Angel Rejects*. The concept's a winner," Melodie declared. "It's a blend of a talent quest, a reality show, and angels."

"I've heard enough," said Bob, winking at me.

He left, followed by Lonnie, who said to me on the way out, "She's all yours."

Melodie frowned at his retreating back. "I can't be too hard on Lonnie. I guess he always wanted to be a star himself." She spread her hands. "But he hasn't got it, know what I mean?"

"I'll look after the phone for you."

She wasn't listening. "If I don't get a call-back—though Larry says the part of Angelique is made for me—then I'll do the open call with the bees."

"Bees?"

"That's my name for them. The would-be if you could-be people. Like, everyone from Kansas who thinks they'll find fame and fortune in the big city. Open call means anyone can turn up to try out, but it's not for the main parts."

"Isn't that the phone?"

"Oh, rats!" Melodie sprinted down the corridor.

After making my tea, I collected my shoulder bag and, mug in hand, followed Melodie to the reception area. In my bag my bookstore purchase was safely concealed. I'd been planning to study it tonight, but if I was going to be discussing my undercover role over dinner, I needed a quick squiz at it now. It was important to be on top of things.

I found Melodie seated behind the desk, trying her persuasive techniques on the phone. "Oh, come on, Tiffany. You can take some time off. No one will know. I'm only asking for a couple of hours. This is my big chance!"

Clearly Tiffany was not cooperating, as after a few more entreaties Melodie sighed, said goodbye, and put down the phone.

"It's not as if she's got the kind of job that keeps her chained to a desk," she said to me.

"What's Tiffany do?" I asked.

Melodie pouted. "She's a professional gift buyer. Like, she could take time off *easily*."

"What's a professional gift buyer?"

"Tiffany works for Superior Gifts Plus. She shops for stars but never meets them. Like, the movie studios, the producers, and the talent agencies all give gifts to their actors on special occasions like the start of a new movie, or an Oscar nomination, or signing a big contract."

"She gets paid for buying presents for people?"

Melodie nodded. "The sky's the limit. Tiffany can spend what she likes. The studios spend millions of dollars on gifts for talent throughout the year. Someone's got to buy them. That's where Tiffany and Superior Gifts Plus comes in."

"I'd never do that job," I said. "I'm not all that keen on shopping."

Melodie's eyes widened. "You're not?" She considered my failure in this area for a moment, then, recalling her situation, said mournfully, "Tiffany was my last hope."

"I'll answer the phone for you this arvo." When she looked puzzled, I translated. "Afternoon. The phone. I'll answer it."

Transformed, she leapt to her feet. "You will! Oh, Kylie, I owe you one!" Apparently fearful I might change my mind, she grabbed her things and galloped for the front door.

"You're leaving already?" I called, but she was gone.

I settled down with my book, keeping a *Hollywood Reporter* handy to conceal it should anyone come along. I'd be red-faced if people—well, Ariana mainly—thought I needed extra help, but it couldn't hurt to do some studying on the side.

Several calls came through, but the phone set-up was chick-enfeed compared to the pub, so I aced it without any prob. I put a call through to Bob, and he chuckled when he heard my voice. "Melodie won out, did she? Watch out, Kylie, this won't be the last time she asks you."

I was really into a chapter on industrial espionage when a voice said, "Whatcha reading?"

I closed my book and covered the title with my hand. "Nothing."

"Looks like something to me." It was a delivery bloke in a daggy outfit of brown shorts and shirt. He slapped the package he was carrying down on the desk and gave me an overly famil-iar smile. "Where's Melodie? Auditioning again?"

"That's right."

He was one of those mega-annoying friendly types who can't mind their own business. "Good book?" he asked. "I'm a reader myself. Spy stuff. Techno-thrillers. Tom Clancy. Read him?"

"Not lately."

"You should." Before I could react, the twerp had reached over and grabbed my book. "Well, well," he said, grinning. He read the title in a loud voice. "*Private Investigation: The Complete Handbook.*"

"Give me that!" I snatched it back from him.

Too late. Fran was on the scene. And she was smiling.

TWELVE

"I'm throwing myself on your mercy," I said, shoving the book into my bag.

"Oh, yeah?" Fran was still smirking.

I looked around. The coast was clear. The delivery bloke had left, whistling cheerfully, not giving a thought to the fact he'd given Fran a weapon to king-hit me with.

"You know how you've aced this gofering thing..." I began.

Fran's smile vanished as though it had never existed. "What? What thing?"

"Ariana said you were a gofer, so I suppose when you're doing it, you're gofering."

It was impossible, but her hair seemed to suddenly flame a deeper red. "I'm not a gofer," she ground out. "I'm the office manager."

"Good-oh. Well, you know how you've aced this office managering thing?"

Fran narrowed her eyes to slits. "Yes?" she said, drawing the word out.

I was going to have to be a real bullshit artist to pull this one off, but I'd give it a go. "It's sort of like you're an inspiration to me. I want to ace private-eyeing the way you ace your job. That's why I'm studying on the sly. Don't want anyone to think I'm not a natural at this P.I. stuff."

I paused to see the effect of my words. Not encouraging. Fran wasn't frowning, but she wasn't looking receptive either. Blast her. I wasn't going to beg.

"Let me put it this way, Fran. I'd be really embarrassed if it got out I was reading a book on how to be a P.I. So I'm asking you to forget you saw it."

"Okay."

"Okay? You won't say anything?"

"Not a word. But you owe me. And believe it, I'll collect."

The front door opened, and in came a tallish bloke wearing ancient jeans and a red T-shirt with the words SLOW-SLOW FAST-FAST across the front in purple letters. He didn't fit Melodie's description of intense, having a putty face and a blob of a nose, although I noticed in contrast his thin-lipped mouth was set in a hard line. I took a punt and said, "G'day. You'd be Rich Westholme."

He glared at me suspiciously. "Who told you that?"

"She's training to be a P.I.," said Fran, with a touch of malice.

I indicated his chest. "Melodie mentioned that was the title of one of your movies."

His dark frown lightened. "Yeah," he said. "You can catch it on cable next month."

Julia Roberts came stalking down the hallway, then leapt with great grace up on the desk. He recoiled. "Jesus, get her away from me."

Jules, sensing someone who was repulsed by her feline self, walked delicately in his direction. I took pity on him, scooped her up, and deposited her on my side of the desk. She gave me a disgusted glare, then walked off, her tail snapping with irritation.

"Thanks. I can't stand cats." Rich Westholme peered around as though Melodie might be crouching beneath the desk. "Melodie here?"

"Audition," said Fran. She put her hands on her hips, which

shoved her spectacular bosom out another centimeter or so. "You've missed her."

I got the impression she'd taken an instant dislike to Westholme, though with Fran it was hard to tell. She didn't look on anyone with much approval.

On the other hand, Rich Westholme was giving Fran, and her bosom, the glad eye. "Call me Rich. And you are...?"

"Not available."

He laughed, apparently thinking she was joking. "Good one. No, seriously, what's your name?"

"Fran," I said. "She's our office manager."

"Watch it," said Fran to me.

Rich Westholme slapped on a slimy smile. "Well, Fran, have you ever thought of being in movies?"

She directed a look at him I thought might burn his sallow face, but he continued to grin at her.

"What about me?" I said. "Maybe I've got ambitions to be in movies."

"Yeah, yeah." He didn't even bother looking in my direction. To Fran he said, "I'm casting at the moment. There could be a part for you."

I winced as Fran opened her rosebud mouth, having a fair idea what her response was going to be. With terrific timing, Melodie blew through the door at this exact instant. "Rich!" She rushed over and planted a proprietary kiss on his cheek. "You didn't say you were coming by."

"Yeah, well, I was in the neighborhood."

The phone rang. I waited to see if Melodie was intending to resume her duties, but she was too busy looping her arm through Rich's and leading him off. "Honey, you said you wanted to see where I work, so let me give you the official tour. And you'll want to hear about my audition..."

Fran said, "Dickhead."
I said, "Fuckwit."
We looked at each other. "You're all right," said Fran.

⊃

I was excited but not showing it. I'd expected we have dinner in some local restaurant, but instead we were going to Ariana's place. Bob Verritt was driving and I was playing it cool. He was negotiating the sharp bends of the ascending Hollywood Hills road with more smooth skill than I had shown this morning. Of course, Bob probably had the advantage of knowing exactly where he was going. "Have you been to Ariana's place many times?"

His long face split in a smile. "Not often, and every time it's like receiving an invitation from the queen."

"She lives alone, doesn't she?"

"Apart from Gussie."

An arrow of disappointment skewered me. Then I thought how stupid I was to have thought otherwise. Why would someone as attractive as Ariana be alone?

"Here we are." Bob pulled through an entryway into a small-ish parking lot just off the road. There was room for three, maybe four cars. A barred gate began sliding across to secure the area from the road. Facing us was the door of a double garage, and I supposed Ariana's BMW was nestling in there side-by-side with whatever Gussie drove. I pictured something sporty—maybe even a Porsche.

Not much could be seen of Ariana's house from this vantage point, just a blank wall with an entrance door. "Smile," said Bob, "you're on *Candid Camera*."

I looked more carefully at the entrance. "There's a surveillance camera here?"

"Don't bother looking—you won't find it. The lens is tiny."

I became aware of a deep barking. The dog wasn't hysterical, but merely well-mannered, announcing there were intruders on the premises.

Ariana opened the door, her left hand hooked into the collar of a large German Shepherd. "Don't mind Gussie. She's friendly, as long as you don't attack me."

Gussie, tongue lolling, checked out Bob, gave a quick wave of her tail to acknowledge she recognized him, then switched her watchful gaze to me. I could have flung my arms around her neck and hugged her but thought it better to be more circumspect. Besides, I know dogs well, and although she seemed friendly, her role was to guard Ariana, and I was a stranger.

Ariana stood aside to let us in. "I got Chinese takeout. I hope that's okay."

"Bonzer." I realized I'd skipped lunch. "I'm starving."

"Then let's eat first and work later."

The house was on three levels, the last being a living room that stretched the entire length of the building. Jarrod Perkins could not have had a more stunning view. Far below us the brilliant lights of the city stretched in sparkling patterns until they reached a darkness I presumed was the Pacific Ocean. How odd to think the waves of that same ocean beat upon the shores of my own country, half a world away.

I'd expected the decor of Ariana's house to be stark, perhaps with black and white predominating, like her office. I couldn't have been more wrong. It was warm, comfortable, and welcoming. The walls were pale cream, the polished wooden floors glowed with honey tints, the couches and chairs, arranged to take advantage of the view, were upholstered in a deep rose fabric.

I would have loved to have had a tour of the whole house, but

Ariana ushered us into a dining area adjacent to the kitchen, where we could look at the city lights while we ate.

Gussie stationed herself nearby, keeping an eye on Bob and me. I grinned at her. "You may look fierce, but you're just a big, gorgeous sook," I said. She cocked her head, considering me, then flapped her plumed tail a couple of times.

Fortunately Ariana had ordered generously. While she picked at her food and Bob ate moderately, I feasted. Takeaway from Wong's Café in the 'Gudge ran a pretty poor second to this spread. And just like I'd seen in the movies, everything came in delightful little cardboard containers that folded over at the top, not the plastic trays I was accustomed to.

"That was beaut," I said, sitting back with a sigh of satisfaction. "Thank you."

We moved to the living room for coffee. "I'm afraid I'm a poor host," Ariana told me. "I don't have loose tea, but I do have Twinings tea bags. Could you slum, just this once?" She almost smiled as she added, "It's not the herbal tea you so dislike."

I said I'd have coffee, but I was charmed by the offer. Almost as charmed as I was by the house, but nowhere near how much I was charmed by Ariana Creeling herself.

When we moved to the living room, Gussie came too, putting herself beside Ariana's chair. Bob folded himself onto one of the couches, and I sat beside him.

Ariana was all business. "Bob, what's the report on the Challoner case?"

He groaned. "Tracking this particular missing teenager is no piece of cake, especially when her parents are in the middle of an acrimonious divorce and blaming each other for their daughter's disappearance. Add to that the girl took quite a sum of money with her, and she's got an excellent support group. Getting information out of her friends is like pulling teeth, but I'm getting there, slowly but surely."

They discussed the runaway Cassie Challoner for a few minutes, then Ariana said to me, "Let's get to the Deerdoc situation."

"The Hummer?"

"It was an incendiary device. No details yet. Perkins made it easy, as he never bothers to lock his vehicles. The doorman of the building didn't notice anything, but it could have been planted long before Perkins parked the Hummer in Beverly Hills. When he was interviewed by the cops this afternoon, he said he had no idea who could have wanted to harm him."

"Ha!" Bob snorted. "If you included everyone Jarrod Perkins has pissed off, potential suspects would number in the thousands."

"Do you think the bomb has anything to do with the missing therapy session recordings?" I asked.

"It's possible," said Ariana. "I did my best to persuade Dave Deer to tell the police about the blackmail threat, but he insists it's got to be kept quiet."

Bob said, "You don't believe they're one and the same? The thief is the blackmailer?"

"It would be very helpful if it were one person, but I've a strong feeling it isn't the case."

Bob grinned at me. Jerking his thumb at Ariana, he said, "Always trust this one's strong feelings. She's uncanny. Spooky, even."

"Just don't call it female intuition," said Ariana. She handed us stapled pages. "Lonnie and Harriet have completed background checks of the staff. These four have been less than frank, as you'll see. Even so, Kylie, when you're at Deerdoc don't concentrate only on these people. In my experience it often turns out to be the last one you'd expect."

"Like the butler," I piped in.

"There are butlers in Hollywood," said Bob. "The most highly prized specimens speak with that lockjaw English accent. Jarrod Perkins doesn't have one, however. His personal assistant, Sven, fills the role of butler, troubleshooter, bodyguard, enforcer. The whole enchilada."

"How do you know all this?" I asked.

"I've done work for Perkins in the past. Never again. He's an asshole of the first order."

I studied the names of those meriting closer attention: Reuben Kowalski, Randy Romaine, Kristi Jane Russo, and Oscar Sherwood.

I was about to comment if you called someone randy in Australia you would mean they were oversexed, but then I decided this would be entirely too flippant. "How about Deer's personal assistant?" I asked. "Noreen resigned awfully fast today. Maybe she's bailing before she's caught."

Ariana considered this, absently stroking Gussie's head. "Her background checks out, but you could be right. I'll have Harriet take another look at her."

Bob gave me advice for my undercover role. The golden rule, he told me, was to avoid confrontation. "Let's say you catch someone red-handed doing something incriminating, get out of there and call security. Don't try and handle it yourself."

"In this case security's Fred Mills," I said. "He could be worse than nothing."

"You work with what you've got," said Bob.

"Whoopy-do," I said, unimpressed.

"Because you're new, no one's going to be surprised if you ask a lot of questions, but be careful not to overdo it, and always have a convincing reason for asking the question, in case you're challenged."

"I'm a natural stickybeak. How about that?"

Bob patted my shoulder. "With that cute accent of yours, I'm guessing you can ask as many questions as you like."

We spent the next half hour going through the shortlist. Reuben Kowalski had neglected to advise he had an extensive arrest record, spread over several states, for petty theft. Randy Romaine hadn't found it necessary to mention his hobby of celebrity stalking. He'd been picked up several times late at night loitering outside female stars' homes, and in two instances he'd actually trespassed. Kristi Jane Russo was an Aussie with a drinking problem she'd concealed in her job application. In Sydney she'd been involved in two serious traffic accidents, one with fatalities. Oscar Sherwood had never been charged with anything, but in two of his previous jobs considerable sums of money had mysteriously disappeared.

"These four have no idea we have this information," said Ariana. "We don't want to tip them off. After this is over, however, I don't believe they can count on continuing their careers at Deerdoc."

I looked down at Gussie, who had her head resting on her paws but her eyes fixed hopefully on Ariana. "Is she waiting for her walk?"

"I take her every night."

"But she doesn't have a yard, does she? Why don't you bring her down to the office during the day?"

Bob grinned. Ariana sighed. "I'm touched you're worried about Gussie's welfare," she said crisply. "Would it make you feel better to know I have a professional handler who picks Gussie up each weekday, along with a number of other dogs, and takes them running at a dog park?"

"It does make me feel better."

"Is there anything else I can help you with?"

She was being sarcastic, of course, but if Bob hadn't been there maybe I'd have said "Too right, there is!" and leaned over and kissed her.

Or maybe not. Okay, definitely not. But crikey, it was tempting...

THIRTEEN

I put on the car radio while driving to Beverly Hills for my first proper day's work at Deerdoc. Jarrod Perkins was still the lead news item, popping up everywhere and never missing a chance to plug his latest project, a movie called *Primitive Obsessions*.

Last night Jules and I had picked up some of the frenzy about Jarrod Perkins on the late TV news, and the story was still going strong this morning. In the kitchen Fran had the teev turned up high. There'd been lots of angles of the Hummer's burning wreckage, breathless theories floated about who might conceivably be responsible—Homeland Security was hinting at an Al Qaeda terrorist cell—and roving reporters shoving microphones under the noses of local residents, who had been variously shocked, horrified, or oddly pleased about the bomb blast in their exclusive area. Unlike Aussies, these people never seemed to get tongue-tied but burbled on freely as soon as the media appeared.

"They'll never eat lunch in this town again," Fran had observed. She'd taken another bite from a ghastly-looking health food bar. "Beverly Hills doesn't forgive."

"What do you mean?"

"It's not done, talking to a reporter in the street. A studio interview, though, would be okay."

I'd been given directions to Noreen's car spot under the building, where there were three floors of parking. The patients had the first floor, the doctors the second, and the rest of the staff was relegated to the bottom parking area.

I didn't have a keycard yet, so I stopped beside the attendant sitting in his little box. He was a middle-aged bloke in a creased uniform who'd quickly hidden the magazine he was reading when I'd pulled up. Without even asking my name, he raised the arm and waved me through.

"Aren't you going to ask who I am? I could be a terrorist, deadset on blowing up the building."

He gave me a long look, a bit like Ariana's specialty but not nearly as effective. "Are you a terrorist?" he finally asked.

"No."

"Are you intending to blow up the building?"

"Not today."

Weary sigh. "Then go on through."

"Do you *ever* ask people questions, or is it open slather and anyone can get in?"

Another sigh. "If you look suspicious, lady, I ask. You don't look suspicious."

This wasn't good enough. I'd be reporting a security breach in the parking structure. "You know Fred Mills?" I said.

"Great guy. I count him as a friend. Why?"

"Just asking."

I located Noreen's parking spot without too much trouble. It was on the lowest floor, but at least it wasn't too far from the lift. I punched the up button. By the time it arrived, a crowd had formed behind me. It seemed everyone was clutching a carton of coffee or one of those insulated mug things. I got swept up as everybody squeezed into the lift.

As the door closed, I twisted my neck trying to find the

notice that gave the maximum load for this particular lift, but it was blocked by bodies. I was visualizing the horror of being stuck between floors with this lot when the door opened and everyone spilled out. There'd been total silence for the short journey, except for one bloke who'd whistled "Oklahoma" under his breath and out of tune. Released from confinement, everyone started talking as they scattered toward their work stations.

Chantelle was already at her post. "Good morning, Kylie."

"Good morning, Chantelle. What's the good oil?" She seemed to need more, so I added, "What's going on? Anything interesting?"

"Not yet. The day is young."

I gave her a big grin. I really liked this woman's attitude. In fact, when I thought about it, Chantelle herself wasn't bad at all. She had lovely dark skin and beautiful hands. And her red mouth was, frankly, alluring.

"Alluring" was the last thing that came to mind where Fred Mills was concerned. He was waiting in Dave Deer's office, bubbling with impatience. "I'm a busy man, so this briefing can only take a few minutes of my time."

"You should know the bloke at the parking entrance let me through without asking any questions."

"So what?"

"I could have been anybody. I could have had a bomb in the boot."

He flapped a hand at me. "Yeah, yeah. I'll check it out."

If possible, Fred looked even less appetizing than the last time I'd seen him, so I concentrated on the surroundings. Dave Deer's office was the max in luxury. The white carpet was so thick you could turn your ankle if you weren't careful. The paintings hanging on the paneled walls were obviously originals, each subtly illuminated with recessed lighting. The furniture was sleek, with lots of chrome. The desk was perfectly clear.

The office had three rich, polished doors. I'd entered through one from the main office area. Another was ajar, and I could see it led to a private bathroom. I was guessing the third door would open into a black-and-white therapy room.

I became aware Fred was speaking: "...go it alone."

"You want me to go it alone?"

This earned me an exasperated grunt. "That's exactly want I *don't* want you to do. I've already pointed out that you're an amateur, way out of your depth. I don't want to rush around rescuing you from situations you've got yourself into. Low profile. Say that to yourself often. Low profile."

"Low profile. Got it." I couldn't resist adding, "But Fred, if I holler...?"

A sneer of superiority distorted his upper lip. "I'll be there, little lady, I'll be there."

I didn't need to holler for help even once during the day. Dave Deer was in San Diego, addressing a mental health symposium, so I was free to wander around meeting people and getting the lay of the land.

First I went down to the entrance of the building and made myself known to the doorman, Jim, and the guard in the lobby, Malcolm. I reckoned this was a good move, so that in case I needed a favor, these blokes would be on side.

My fun discovery of the day was Irma Barber, who was at serious odds with the dress standards adhered to by the most of the Deerdoc staff. Irma was wearing khaki pants, the sort with lots of unnecessary pockets everywhere, and Birkenstocks with striped socks. Her T-shirt proclaimed CHICKENS RULE over the picture of a cartoon chook. I didn't get the point at all and concluded it was some American thing.

Noticing my fascinated gaze, Irma laughed. "As you can imagine, I'm not allowed where the public or the patients can see me. I work behind the scenes with Oscar, keeping all the office equipment humming along."

Oscar had to be Oscar Sherwood, who'd left previous jobs under a cloud because of missing money, although he'd never been formally charged. He was Deerdoc's resident techo, who, as Irma said, kept everything electronic in the office, including the computer network, working smoothly. One of his duties was making sure each therapy session had an audiovisual record, so he was automatically a possible suspect for the theft of the disks.

Last night I'd argued to Ariana and Bob that he couldn't be the one, because with his knowledge he'd make a copy, not take the disks from the file. Or he could simply send the information to a distant computer using the Internet. While I'd been speaking, however, it had begun to dawn on me that maybe Sherwood intended for suspicion to fall on someone not technologically adept. And if the disks weren't missing from the files there would be no concrete proof blackmail material had been taken.

Irma introduced me to Sherwood in the manner of an indulgent mother showing off a talented child. Oscar Sherwood was young enough to make me feel like an older woman. His face made him look about fifteen, but a powerful fifteen. The muscles in his arms were truly impressive, and he wore an extremely tight sleeveless top to allow appreciation of his toned torso.

"Hi," he said, preoccupied with the innards of a copying machine.

"G'day."

"Filling in for Noreen?"

"That's right."

"Good luck."

Leaving him diving deeper into the mechanism, with Irma handing him tools when needed, I wandered off to explore further.

Deerdoc Enterprises was clearly a thriving corporation, leasing the entire three-floor building on Roxbury Drive. Dave Deer's Slap! Slap! Get On With It therapy room was on the middle floor, adjacent to his office. It had two entrances: one directly from his office, and one leading to a private corridor. The room was exactly as it had appeared in the demonstration disk and was, I discovered, one of three such black-and-white rooms. I peered closely at the white carpet, wondering if the hearty slaps delivered during treatment ever caused a nosebleed, but the thick pile was stain-free.

Next I checked out the walk-in safe where the theft had taken place. It had an electronic lock requiring a keycard to open it. I didn't have one, but that wasn't a problem, as the door wasn't shut. Inside were ranks of shallow drawers, all neatly labeled in alphabetical order. They had no locking mechanism, so I pulled one out to examine the contents. Patients had individual heavy plastic files, each with the name clearly shown. I pulled out another drawer. Stone the crows! Famous name after famous name jumped out at me. This was a blackmailer's heaven.

A bloke in a white coat came in, looking preoccupied. He paid absolutely no attention to me, going to one of the drawers and extracting a file. He was wearing a badge indicating he was Dr. Walter Yeats.

"G'day, Dr. Yeats."

"Mmmm? Oh, hi."

"I could be anyone, you know."

He looked up from the file, focused on me, and said soothingly, "I'm sure you can be. Ambition is a wonderful motor to power one's life."

"I don't mean that. I mean I could be an intruder, deadset on stealing files."

"Have you often felt this sense of alienation?"

"I'm not a patient."

"Of course not." He tucked the file he'd extracted under one arm, reached into the pocket of his white coat, extracted a business card, and pressed it into my hand. "If you feel the necessity to talk, please don't hesitate to call. Anytime."

A comforting pat on my shoulder and he was gone. Crikey! I knew the staff hadn't been told about the missing disks, so there was no security flap going on, but even so this was past a joke. If the fancy took me, there'd be nothing to stop me from helping myself to an armful of files and skedaddling with them.

I set off to run down the remaining three high-level suspects. Working on the principle that everyone eventually would end up in the staff dining area, if only for a cup of coffee, I staked it out around lunchtime—lurking, I hoped inconspicuously, by a staff notice board. It was a good move: In a few minutes I had a meeting with both Kristi Jane Russo of the PR department and Randy Romaine of Accounting.

Kristi Jane was one of those people who always talk too loudly, so I heard her long before I saw her. In her broad Aussie accent, she was yelling, "Keith's got the bloody hide of a bloody elephant. He says to me, 'Now, listen, Kristi Jane,' and I say to him, 'I'm fed up with listening. I want action.' And Randy, you just won't believe what he says to me then..."

I was betting this Randy would be Randy Romaine. I waited with keen interest for the pair to come around the corner. In a moment they did. Kristi Jane's voice proved to be much bigger than her body. She had the slight, flat-chested physique of a thin young girl, bizarrely topped by an exaggerated bouffant hairdo.

Randy Romaine looked like an accountant, which was what

he was. Fittingly, perhaps, he was monochrome: brown hair, brown eyes, brown suit, brown shoes. He had a forgettable face and restrained body language. He certainly didn't fit my mental picture of a stalker. Perhaps he'd reformed and was leading a blameless life, with his stalking days behind him. Or perhaps he'd merely put his stalking on hold and was cultivating the new field of blackmail.

"G'day," I said, practically leaping in front of them. I beamed at Kristi Jane. "I couldn't help hearing your accent. I'm an Aussie too. I'm just filling in as Dr. Deer's assistant for the next few weeks."

That broke the ice. "Did you hear why Noreen resigned?" bellowed Kristi Jane. "Terrorism! You've got to stand up to the bastards. Noreen's a lily-livered little twit!" In a moment she'd swept me up into her conversation and into the dining room, where she bullied a mousy bloke into giving up his spot at a table and installed Randy, herself, and me in his place.

Apart from the desire I had to pop earplugs into my ears to mute Kristi Jane's deafening voice, I quite enjoyed myself. She was a mine of information as far as company gossip was concerned, and better still she wasn't a bit reticent about it.

Randy Romaine turned out to have a very dry sense of humor, which went rather well with his quiet demeanor. I tried but couldn't find any real distinguishing feature. The bloke was pleasant but not memorable. I did notice, however, how thick his neck was. "Do you work out?" I asked.

"Why, yes."

"*Do* you?" Kristi Jane regarded him with surprised irritation. "I never knew that. Why didn't you tell me?"

So by mid afternoon I had three down and one to go— Reuben Kowalski. I found Kristi Jane in the PR department shouting into a phone. When she'd finished, I said, "Dr. Deer told me to speak with Reuben Kowalski. He's supposed to be in the billing department, but I can't find him."

"That's because the bastard will be outside the building, smoking. Bloody pathetic, don't you think? Not being able to give up an addiction that's going to kill you is pretty piss-weak."

She added I couldn't miss him as he'd be the only one wearing a purple shirt. "Always wears purple, and he's not even bloody gay," she advised. I thanked her, wondering if Kristi Jane had defeated her own addiction to alcohol.

Reuben Kowalski was exactly where she said he'd be. Los Angeles, I'd been learning, had some of the strictest anti-smoking ordinances in the country, so smokers in office buildings were forced to go outside to avoid inflicting secondhand smoke on colleagues. There was a narrow alleyway running down one side of the building, and a small group of tobacco lepers had congregated there to puff furiously on cigarettes.

I stopped to examine the spot where the Hummer had been destroyed. The road was blackened, but every piece of the twisted remains had been removed, probably for forensic examination.

In the alleyway, Reuben was sucking on a cigarette and talking with great animation on a mobile phone. As Kristi Jane had told me, his shirt was deep purple, and oddly enough this color seemed to suit him. He had tight curly hair turning gray and a droopy, nicotine-stained mustache.

I'd manufactured a reason to see him—a billing that had supposedly gone astray. I introduced myself. Playing anxious-to-please temporary worker, I said, "So sorry to interrupt you, Mr. Kowalski, but Dr. Deer will be calling this afternoon about this matter and..." I let my voice trail off and sloped my eyebrows the wrong way.

He took a final mighty suck of his cigarette. "Okay, I'll come in now."

"Oh, thank you, Mr. Kowalski."

Melodie might have done a better job, but I had to admit I quite impressed myself. Not to skite, but I wasn't half bad at this acting routine. And now I'd accomplished step one, which was to establish casual contact with the suspects, I could keep up the act by getting them to accept me as just another member of the Deerdoc staff.

I left at five so I could catch Ariana in the office and give her my first day's report. I felt a bit guilty leaving early, which was stupid, as I wasn't really Dave Deer's personal assistant. I wasn't going to sneak around, so I said "Good night, Chantelle" as I passed her on the way out.

"Hold on a moment, Kylie."

I came back to her desk, ready to argue I could leave the premises when I wished. She said, "I've got tickets for a play Friday night. It's a little local theater. I was wondering if you'd like to come with me."

I wasn't lost for words often. This was one of the times. "Um," I said.

Chantelle chuckled. "Yes, it's a date. I'm asking you on a date. Think it over and tell me tomorrow. Or you can call me." She passed me a Deerdoc business card. "My cell number's on the back."

"Right-oh."

I rode down to the parking structure deep in thought. I was looking at Chantelle in an entirely different light. It was rather flattering to be asked, I told myself, but how did she know..?

"Melodie!" The receptionists' bush telegraph had been at work.

"Excuse me?"

"Oh, sorry," I said to the bloke sharing the lift with me. "I was thinking out loud."

When I got to Kendall & Creeling, I was ridiculously disappointed to find Ariana had left for the day, however Melodie had a consolation prize for me. "You can meet Fran's husband, Quip, if you like. He's in the kitchen talking to Rich."

"Quip? Is that a name?"

"I think it's actually Bruce, but Quip wanted something that'd stand out on the first page of a script. Quip Trent. Comedy writer, so it suits, don't you think?"

"Would I have seen any of his work? Movies? TV?"

Melodie shook her head, a look of deep compassion on her face. "The biz can be so hard. Quip hasn't sold a script yet." She brightened up to add, "Any day now, though. Rich says he might use Quip as a script doctor for his new project."

This was one for the books. "How can Quip be a script doctor if he's never had any of his own scripts made?"

With a forbearing smile, Melodie explained, "You don't get how the biz works. Hardly *any* scripts get made. It's the writing of them that's important."

She broke off as the delivery bloke in the daggy brown outfit—who'd made me feel a real galah yesterday—came in with a pile of boxes. While Melodie was sorting through them, the bloke nudged me in the ribs.

"Well, well," he said, grinning. "Solved any big crimes lately?" He looked me up and down, noted my tailored dress, and chuckled some more. "Dressing for success, are we?"

"I am," I said, "but jeez, look at you."

"What?"

"It's hard to look good in brown. Especially *that* brown." I added, as my exit line, "It's cruel, really, making you wear that uniform."

"Hey, wait a minute..."

I strode off, mad as a cut snake. This blasted bloke would tell

Melodie how he found me reading *Private Investigation: The Complete Handbook.* This news would hit the receptionists' telegraph. Soon everyone would know. Including Ariana.

There were four people in the kitchen: Lonnie, clutching his ever-present mug of coffee; Rich Westholme, lounging against the counter; Fran, frowning; and someone who must be Quip.

His handsome face lit with amusement, he was saying, "Oh, my God, I saw Molly Ringwald the other day. I mean, *hi,* can we say blast from the past? I mean, what has she done since *Pretty in Pink?* Hello!"

This bloke had to be gay. He was everything I loved in a man: humorous, delightful, and homosexual.

A hot glare from Fran caught my attention. "He's mine," she said. "Keep your paws off him. I won't say it twice."

FOURTEEN

Early next morning I was explaining to Julia Roberts how she'd have to keep a stiff upper lip because I'd be gone again today, when Ariana knocked on my door. Fortunately I'd made the bed and everything was tidy.

Ariana stood in the doorway, wearing her signature black. Her pale hair was as smooth as her expressionless face. It mystified me how she projected that aura of cool, contained authority without appearing to do anything at all. My imagination skittered around, trying to visualize her in the depths of passion. Before I got to the point of short-circuiting, Ariana said, "I tried to get you on your cell phone, but no luck."

"Sorry, I didn't think anyone knew the number to ring me, so I didn't turn it on." I went over to my bag, retrieved the phone, and activated it. "Hey, now that I know *you* have the number, it'll be on twenty-four-seven, no worries."

"Tell me about yesterday."

I gave her a complete rundown, including my assessment of how crook the security at Deerdoc was.

She listened without comment, then said, "Dave Deer called last night. He wants to know when you're moving in."

"I'm not."

"Why? Is it leaving Julia Roberts that's holding you back?"

"It's that Dave Deer's a lech. If I move in there, sooner or later Elise is going to catch him putting the hard word on me. It'd be a nasty sitch."

"What makes you think you won't face the same situation in the office?"

"Look, Ariana, I know he's our client, and he's an important one. I'll do my best to make sure it doesn't happen, but he can't cop a free feel and not have me get snarky about it."

"Just so long as you don't throw him over your shoulder, as I recall you did the captain of the football team."

I blushed a bit, remembering how I'd boasted about that the first day we'd met. "Hell's bells," I said. "Do you remember everything?"

"Everything."

"I'd better be careful what I say."

When a ringing sound started, I looked around, puzzled. "Your cell phone," said Ariana.

It was Chantelle. "Have you decided about Friday?"

I didn't ask how she'd got my number. I knew. "You could have asked me at work," I said, aware Ariana, who'd moved to stroke Jules, couldn't help overhearing my end of the conversation.

Chantelle's chuckle was warm and promising. "I couldn't wait."

"Okay, I accept."

"Terrific. See you soon."

The mobile gave a discreet burp when I ended the call. "Someone from work has tickets for a play," I said, feeling the need to explain.

"I hope not on Saturday night."

"No, Friday. Why?"

"You mentioned you'd like to see my sister's work. The

gallery has a private showing of Janette's new exhibition this Saturday night."

Now, this wasn't a date, not really, but I still felt a tingle of excitement. "That'd be great, Ariana."

Crikey, I was even getting a charge out of saying Ariana's name. I mentally tried *Chantelle*. Bit of a jolt, but not as much. I frowned to myself. This was rebound stuff. I couldn't say, or even think, Raylene's name without a pang. Overcompensating, that's what it was. I was trying to fill the void she'd left with other women. Maybe I needed some Slap! Slap! Get On With It therapy. Or maybe I just needed some good, healthy, uncomplicated sex.

"What in the world are you thinking about?" Ariana asked.

"Nothing in particular. Why?"

She shook her head, smiled at me, said, "Again, Kylie, you find me lost for words."

She went off, still shaking her head, bemused. I consoled myself with the thought that I had some effect on Ariana, even if it wasn't quite the one I would have hoped.

My mobile rang again. This time it was Melodie. "Kylie, I've got a favor to ask, and you'll probably be gone before I get to work."

"I can't look after the phone."

"It's not the phone. It's something else...a big favor, actually. I'll understand if you say no."

She wouldn't, of course. "What is it?"

"In the top drawer of my desk there's an envelope with head and shoulders."

"Yes?" I said doubtfully.

"You know what I mean. My publicity shots. I want you to take one to Deerdoc with you."

"Why?"

"Chantelle called and said Lorelei Stevens has an appointment with Dr. Deer this morning. I'm sure you'll be seeing her. I'm only asking a little thing. All I want you to do is ask her to autograph my photo."

I didn't bother inquiring how she knew about the appointment. The world of spies could learn a lot from receptionists. "Let me get this straight. You want me to ask Lorelei Stevens to put *her* autograph on *your* photo?"

"If it isn't too much trouble. It's the recognition factor, you see. When Lorelei and I meet in the future, my face will be familiar to her."

"And are you likely to meet Lorelei Stevens in the future?"

"Oh, yes," said Melodie. "I've got an audition. It's a movie where she's the lead, *Heart of Pain.* Larry says I'm just made for the role..."

つ

Fair dinkum, I was astonished. My mum would say gobsmacked. Lorelei Stevens signed Melodie's photo! She didn't even blink or ask who the hell this dame was. She just scrawled her signature right across Melodie's face. And she smiled while she did it.

Of course, she'd been smiling since she came out of the therapy room, both cheeks a bit pink and eyes a bit watery.

A couple of minutes later Dave Deer appeared, his white medical coat so starched it practically crackled. He purred, "Lorelei, we've achieved so much today. You've been very brave. Very brave. But a wise soul like yours knows pleasure comes through pain."

This sounded like S/M to me, but I reckoned neither of them would thank me for sharing that thought, so I didn't. Instead I'd whipped out Melodie's photo and asked the film star to sign it.

This particular celebrity was the exception to the blond rule. She was a sultry brunet with aquamarine eyes—I suspected tinted contact lenses—and an astonishing cleavage.

"Alert Ms. Stevens's limo driver she's on the way down," commanded Dave. I called Jim, the doorman, who would signal the limousine driver. If all went according to plan, her luxury transport would draw up just as Dr. Deer and his famous patient exited the building through a special side entrance reserved for celebrities.

Another dazzling smile from Lorelei, and she was gone in a swirl of perfume and stardom. I'd been brushed by fame.

As soon as I'd arrived this morning I'd been taken through the session routine. Before each patient arrived, Oscar Sherwood double-checked the recording equipment. The moment the session ended, the therapist removed the disk and placed it in the patient's file. The normal procedure was to leave files in the therapist's office. At the end of the day there'd be a pile of them waiting for me to take to the walk-in safe, where I'd put each one in the appropriate drawer.

This wasn't really good enough, having files hanging around all day, where they'd be even less secure than in the open safe. It would be extra work, but I intended to put away each patient's folder as soon as the session ended. If Dave Deer wanted to review something, I'd go and retrieve the file.

Lorelei Stevens had been the first patient of the day, so I hopped up and went to get her file from Dave Deer's desk. It was gone!

I heard a faint click as the door to the therapy room closed. I flew over to open it, only to see the other door of therapy room swinging closed. I had to see who had the file. I bounded across to the second door and cracked it enough to look out.

Disappearing down the private corridor was Randy Romaine,

anonymous accountant, a large manila folder casually tucked under one arm. In it, I had no doubt, was the missing file. He disappeared through another door leading to the main office.

Okay, I had to catch Randy red-handed. But if I nabbed him now, he was sure to come up with some convincing story about how he needed the file for accounting purposes. What I had to do was observe him and see what he did. If Randy hid the file, that might be enough. It would be better, though, if he tried to take it out of the building.

I meandered in the direction of Randy Romaine's cubicle. He was behind his desk, stuffing the manila folder into a battered brown briefcase. It looked like this time he was taking everything, not just therapy disks. I slipped into the cubicle next to his—fortunately empty at the moment—and waited for him to make a move.

"Chantelle?" He was on the phone. "Forward all my calls to Gloria. I'll be out for the rest of the day." He left his cubicle and headed ever so casually in the direction of the lift.

Holy cow! It was time for the little lady to holler. I tried Fred's extension. No answer. I dialed his mobile phone. Got voice-mail. As a last resort, I called the doorman. "Jim? This is Kylie Kendall. Is Fred Mills there?"

"Fred's just stepped outside for a smoke. Want me to get him for you?"

"I can't stay on the line. Promise me you'll give him a message. It's mega important."

"Sure. What is it?"

"Tell Fred it's vital he meets me right now in the parking structure, level three. It's really urgent, Jim. Really, really urgent."

"Will do. Parking, level three. You've got it."

Then I ran like a mad thing through the office, shot past Chantelle, who gave me a startled look, then dramatically slowed when I saw Randy getting into the lift.

He looked surprised, but not alarmed, when I joined him. He hadn't put the briefcase down but was clutching it so hard his knuckles showed white. He'd already pressed the button for the level three parking, and when I didn't punch a button for another floor, he said, "You're leaving early?"

"Dentist."

"A problem?"

"Wisdom tooth."

He nodded. "They can be nasty."

I looked at him sideways. Randy Romaine looked the same as yesterday. A mild, inoffensive accountant. I felt a shiver of alarm. He'd been an amateur stalker, and there were no reports of any harm coming to the objects of his obsession. But maybe he'd done more than stalk and not been caught. A physical confrontation with him would not be a good idea. Fortunately I could leave that to Fred.

With a pinging sound the door opened at level three parking. Randy got out briskly and set off at a good pace. I looked around for Fred, but he wasn't there.

Bloody hell! I had to stall Randy somehow. Once he was driving off, it'd be too late. He looked back at me, puzzled, when I called out, "Randy, wait," and took off after him.

"Look, Kylie, I'm in a hurry."

He'd reached his vehicle, a white Toyota sedan. Just the sort of car I'd expect Randy to drive. He unlocked it with his remote key, opened the door, and tossed his briefcase onto the passenger seat.

Still no Fred. Time to improvise. Randy was parked close to a concrete pillar, so he couldn't fully open the driver's door. Before he could get in, I inserted myself between Randy and the door. He looked at me with amazement. "What the hell are you doing?"

"I wanted to have a word with you, in private."

"I'm in a hurry right now. Some other time."

Where the hell was Fred? I looked over Randy's shoulder,

ready to yell, "This way!" but no ungainly figure in a crumpled uniform appeared.

"Shit," said Randy, "just get out of the way."

He attempted to move me bodily by grasping my upper arms, but I resisted. "I'm thinking of buying a Toyota. Would you advise it?"

"Get the hell out of my way."

Someone slammed a car door and took off in a squeal of tires. This was desperation time. Randy was stronger than I was and was plainly about to shove me to one side and get the evidence safely out of the building.

He wasn't taking me seriously, so I found it easy to reach over and snatch the keys from his hand. He was astounded, more than angry. "Give them back to me!"

He tried to grab them, but I put my hand behind my back. "Randy, we have some things to discuss."

"Like what?"

"Like Lorelei Stevens."

Bad move. His face reddened. Squeezing my shoulder painfully hard, he snarled, "This is so fucking stupid. Stop playing games and give me the keys." When I didn't comply, he slammed me hard against the door. "The keys, you bitch!"

"Don't make me hurt you," I said.

This got an incredulous laugh. "You? Hurt *me*?"

A final, desperate look around convinced me Fred wasn't going to be my knight in shining armor. Everything depended on me.

Randy had really lost it now. My ears rang as he backhanded me. "Keys, or I'll break your arm."

Back in Wollegudgerie, when I was doing my self-defense class at the Police Club, the instructor had said, "If you're about to get creamed, there's no point in being squeamish. You do what you have to do."

Looking at Randy's contorted face, I agreed with the instructor wholeheartedly. I dropped the keys and did my best to kick them under the car. Randy punched me. My nose blossomed with blood.

It was clearly time for the Christmas hold. Back in the 'Gudge, we'd all laughed at the name—Christmas hold equals a handful of nuts—but I wasn't laughing now. Tears were running down my cheeks and my nose was spurting blood.

I squinted, trying to see him clearly, and said, "Randy, you're really asking for it." Helped by the fact he didn't consider me a worthy opponent, I took a deep breath, bent my knees, and grabbed at his crotch. Taking a firm grip, I followed the instructor's advice to pull and twist.

It was astonishing how well it worked. Randy bellowed and fell to his knees, then toppled over—helped, I confess, with a push from me.

The lift pinged. Fred came strolling out, thumbs hooked into his belt. His expression changed as he saw Randy groveling on the floor. He hurried over, saying accusingly, "What did you do to him?"

I indicated my nose. "What did he do to *me*, you mean."

Fred's closer inspection of the groaning Randy brought a glare of disapproval. "Could be permanent damage. That's assault, you know."

I fished around and found a tissue to hold against my bleeding nose. "Take a look at the front seat. Randy's got stuff taken from patient files."

Fred wasn't listening. He'd gotten Randy sitting up and had a solicitous arm around his shoulders.

"Jesus Christ," Fred muttered. "These bloody Aussies."

FIFTEEN

As soon as he realized what had happened, Dave Deer was on the phone in a flash. If I wanted a lesson in the power of the celebrity in L.A., I got it now. Almost simultaneously, it seemed to me, the following arrived: four Beverly Hills cops, two to arrest Randy Romaine for assault and two to hang around asking questions; two lawyers, one representing Dave Deer and Deerdoc, the other to look after the interests of Lorelei Stevens; one high-powered P.R. person for Ms. Stevens—Kristi Jane Russo took over this role for Deerdoc; one physician to the stars, called in urgently by Dave Deer, who immediately announced I was too traumatized to be interviewed by the police at the moment.

This wasn't true. Granted, I had a pounding headache, a rapidly blackening eye, and my nose was throbbing like the billy-oh, but I could have answered questions. "No way are you speaking to the cops!" exclaimed Dave Deer, who'd taken Fred and me into his office to consult with his lawyer. "Miles? What's your take on this?"

Miles, a soft, gray man, steepled his lawyerly hands, sent us all a grave look, and said, "At this stage, the less said the better. In that vein, it would be wise, I believe, to provide Mr. Romaine with legal representation. We don't want him to drag any of your clients into a publicity morass."

Dave went quite white at the thought. "Jesus Christ, Miles. Do it! Do it now!"

The lawyer slid neatly out of the office, hardly disturbing the air as he moved. Creepy!

Considering the lengths I'd gone to on Dave Deer's behalf, he was rather low on the gratitude scale. "Lorelei won't be happy if her name's dragged into this."

"It's not my fault Randy Romaine took that particular file," I protested.

Dave Deer switched his displeasure to Fred Mills. "Why weren't you on the spot? Kylie called for assistance. Where were you?"

Fred, with a mean look in my direction, said, "If she hadn't viciously attacked that guy, I could have kept a lid on the whole thing."

"You'll be next, if you keep that up," I said. It was pleasing to me when a nervous expression crossed his flabby face.

Miles slid back into the room. "Too late. Romaine's singing," he said to Dave. "Warbling like a canary." The hard-boiled language sounded ludicrous in his precise little voice.

"Oh, *fuck!*"

"I suggest we get Ms. Kendall out of here. Keep her incommunicado."

Irritated because I was in pain, I snapped, "I'm here, right here in the room. You can talk directly to me."

Miles's smile was as sincere as a saltwater crocodile's. "So sorry. I didn't mean to offend. You do fully comprehend, I trust, that it would be unwise to speak with the authorities without the presence of an attorney."

"Why not just tell them the truth?"

Miles seemed shocked. "I don't believe you understand the ramifications of what you've just said."

My bedroom at Kendall & Creeling glowed in my mind like a

warm and welcoming refuge. I stood up. "I've got a headache and I'm going home."

After argument about whether or not I should drive, I won out and went down to level three, the scene of my confrontation with Randy. I thought maybe I'd see police tape around the scene, but there was nothing but Randy's white Toyota, waiting patiently for him to return.

Outside the Deerdoc building media vans were already congregating. I zipped by, dark glasses perched on my swollen nose. At times like this I saw the benefits of having a generic vehicle that attracted little attention.

I made the Kendall & Creeling car park with a sense of great relief. The high-powered doctor Dave Deer had called in to see me had prescribed a painkiller and rest. Both sounded good to me.

Melodie shrieked when she saw my face. "Oh, my God! It's worse than Chantelle said! Think you'll need plastic surgery?"

Attracted by the commotion, Fran and Lonnie appeared. "Jeez," said Lonnie. "Do you want a cold pack? There's one in the fridge."

"I'm fine."

For Melodie, that was enough about me. "Kylie, I've got a call-back!"

"That's wonderful news." She didn't notice my lack of enthusiasm.

"It's *Angel Rejects*."

"I can't hear this again," said Lonnie, throwing up his hands. As he walked off, he muttered, "I've had it up to here with angels."

"Run it by us again," said Fran, with a wicked smile.

Melodie took her at her word. "It's like this, see. These angels have been thrown out of heaven. Like, they're in human bodies, and they don't remember they're angels, they think they're contestants in a talent quest. The trick is, no one knows which are angels and which are ordinary people. Angelique—that's me—is sort of the angel liaison between heaven and earth. Isn't a big part yet, but Larry says he's sure Angelique will get more air time later in the series."

"I don't get it."

Melodie sighed. "Oh, it's simple, Fran. Listen up. There's some angels and there's some wanna-bes all mixed together and no one knows who's from heaven and who's from earth. At the end of the show the viewers vote for Angel of the Week. If the one they pick *isn't* an angel, the person loses and goes to hell. If the person *is* an angel, they get fifty thousand dollars and a chance to compete another week. See?"

"Never mind," said Fran. "It'll be canceled anyway."

Really stung, Melodie snapped, "It will *not*. And who are you to criticize? I suppose Quip's going to be a big success. Like, how many scripts has he sold, huh?" She stuck out her fingers and pantomimed counting them off. "Let's see. One script? Two scripts? What's that you say? Oh. *No* scripts."

"Let me at her," said Fran.

⊃

For the first time I was sitting behind the desk in Dad's office, now my office. I'd turned on the computer and was busy checking the zillions of e-mails that had piled up. I hadn't checked my messages since I'd left Australia, and they numbered in the hundreds. A fair portion I instantly deleted, as they were spam. I'd just got rid of the last offer to increase the size of my penis when Ariana knocked at the door.

"How are you feeling?"

"Fair to middling," I said.

"Headache?"

"It's better. I've taken something."

It was a change, having her come into my office, rather than the other way around. "Take a seat?" I said, feeling for once I had the advantage.

"Sure. I've come to report on the situation, but first, you did a great job nailing that guy. Congratulations."

I felt ridiculously pleased. "Thanks."

"Dave Deer's done his best to contain the damage, and so far he's been successful. The wild card in the pack is Randy Romaine. He's still in custody, but he'll make bail tomorrow. The line he's taking with the cops is that he's a great fan of Lorelei Stevens and on an impulse borrowed the file. You attacked him quite unjustifiably, he says, and he was only defending himself when he hit you."

"That bastard."

Ariana half smiled. "The cops didn't buy it. Someone with his record of celebrity stalking is behind the eight ball before he even opens his mouth."

"So what happens now?"

"Bob Verritt found his missing teenager last night in Las Vegas. That means he's available to run a fine-tooth comb over Randy Romaine's life. If Romaine's the blackmailer, which I doubt, he's not about to do anything at the moment, now that the cops have taken an interest in him. It's more likely, however, that Romaine was working for somebody else. Bob's following up on that angle."

She looked at me sympathetically. "That's got to be hurting. Why don't you take it easy, lie down?"

"Can I ask you something?"

"Of course."

There was no easy way to get this out, but I had to know. "Did Melodie tell you I'd been reading a book on how to be a P.I.?"

A faint smile touched her lips. "I believe she did mention something along those lines."

"I knew it! I knew that guy in the brown uniform would blab."

"I don't know why you're worried," said Ariana. "It just shows you're taking the job seriously."

I looked at her closely, thinking she might be having me on.

"I mean it," she said.

"Good-oh."

After Ariana had gone I went to find a mirror to assess the damage. I'd had a quick look in the washroom at Deerdoc, and my face had looked a bit battered but not too bad. The passage of time hadn't helped, I found. The swelling was more pronounced, and my black eye was distinctly blacker.

Today was Wednesday. I wouldn't be presentable by Friday. I was about to call Chantelle when she called me on my cell phone. "How are you? I must have just missed you."

"Lucky you. I look like something out of a horror movie. We'd better cancel Friday."

"You're breaking our date? No way."

That warmed me a little, as I'd looking forward to seeing Chantelle outside her work. Perhaps she was destined to play an important part in my future. I could hope.

Julia Roberts turned out to be my solace for the rest of the day, although Ariana did her share by arranging for a local restaurant to deliver dinner.

On Thursday, Dave Deer asked me to come into Deerdoc to meet the detectives on the case. He put me in his office and advised me not to volunteer anything. I expected Miles the creepy lawyer would be there, but it seemed the heat was off and I could be trusted on my own.

The interview was short. It was clear they were merely going through the motions. After the two cops had gone, Dave Deer smiled at me with a certain smugness. "Kept the lid on it," he said. "The media sniffed around but got nothing. Lorelei is very pleased." He rubbed his hands. "I still need you, Kylie. I'm interviewing for a new personal assistant, but in the meantime..."

He never got to hear my answer. Chantelle appeared at the door. "Dr. Deer? Mr. Perkins insists—"

She was bodily knocked out of the way by Jarrod Perkins. I'd seen plenty of people lose their tempers, but this bloke beat them all. He was literally purple in the face. The moment he saw Dave Deer, he screamed, "You motherfucking bastard!" In one shaking hand he held a crumpled sheet of paper. "Explain this!"

Dave Deer zipped behind the protection of his desk. He put up placating hands. "Jarrod, it's me, your therapist."

"Fuck that for a joke! Some bastard's trying to blackmail me." Perkins stood there panting, poised as if about to attack something or someone.

Chantelle, eyes wide, hovered in the doorway. "I'll get Fred Mills."

I saw it dawning on Dave Deer that this was something that must at all costs be kept quiet. "No, Chantelle. This is a medical matter. Please shut the door and make sure we're not disturbed."

Chantelle caught my eye. "Get out," she mouthed.

It was sweet of her, but I wasn't going.

After the door closed, Dave Deer said soothingly, "Now, Jarrod, sit down and let's discuss what's worrying you."

"You supercilious prick. You knew about this and you didn't tell me." He threw the crumpled page onto the desk. "How long have the recordings been missing? How long have you known, you cocksucker? How long?"

Dave Deer looked so sincere I thought his face would melt. "Jarrod, Jarrod. I was just about to contact you."

Perkins leaned over the desk and grabbed Dave's tie. Although he was a much smaller man, his rage had obviously given him strength. He pulled until Dave Deer, red-faced and choking, was halfway across the desk. Shoving his face with its huge beaky nose into the doctor's, Perkins ground out, "I'll ruin you, Deer, ruin you. When I've finished, there won't be a person in Hollywood who'll touch you with a ten-foot pole."

Released, Dave Deer fell back spluttering. Perkins turned to me. "You!"

"Me?"

"You drove me home."

I nodded warily. Who knew what was coming next?

"Tell that bastard over there I want everything in this building that has anything to do with me packaged up and delivered to my house. Every file, every sheet of paper, every fucking recording of every fucking session I've had here. Got that?"

"Got it."

"And I want *you* to deliver it, tomorrow morning." He cast a look of burning scorn in Dave Deer's direction. "I don't intend to breathe the same air as that fuckwit ever again. Tell him if he comes near me I'll kill him."

Crikey, I believed that. "I could probably have the stuff to you this afternoon," I said helpfully.

"I'm on a night shoot, you stupid bitch. Tomorrow morning at ten."

He snatched up the letter from the desk and stalked out of the office.

Dave Deer cleared his throat. "That went well," he said.

I'd never have suspected he was capable of such irony.

ↄ

Friday morning we took my car, with me driving and Ariana navigating. We were using my car because there was a chance

155

Jarrod Perkins might recognize it as the one I'd given him a lift in last Monday. The way the bloke was at the moment, it was wise to avoid upsetting him, and Ariana's BMW would be a strange vehicle as far as he was concerned.

"Can you believe it was only Monday I gave Jarrod Perkins a lift home?" I said. "It seems to have happened yonks ago."

"You've had an eventful week," said Ariana in her customary dry tone.

"Thanks for coming with me," I said. I was more grateful than she knew. I'd visualized myself going up to the director's Hollywood Hills home and, as I seemed to often do, saying something that got quite the wrong reaction. And Jarrod Perkins totally losing it, and before Sven could intervene, strangling me. That was my first scenario. Then I had him shooting me. Or maybe throwing me over the cliff.

So when Ariana had said, "I'm not going to let you go alone, not after that outburst from Perkins. He's unstable at the best of times," I'd been secretly relieved.

"Good-oh. If you insist," I'd said, nonchalant.

Now we were on the way, driving up one of the steep, ascending streets of the Hollywood Hills. A large envelope containing the material Perkins had demanded was sitting on the backseat. Ariana was beside me, wearing black jeans and a black jacket. I glanced over at her. "You've got a gun, haven't you?"

"I do. And before you ask, yes, I'm licensed to carry a concealed weapon."

I felt a whole lot better knowing she was armed. "Are you a good shot?"

"Adequate."

"So you won't go for a head shot, then." I'd been studying *The Complete Handbook* and had just covered the chapter on the use of deadly force.

Out of the corner of my eye I saw Ariana shake her head. "I'll aim for the torso, if that's your advice." I heard the amusement in her voice.

"What if he's wearing a bulletproof vest?"

I actually got a chuckle. "Highly unlikely."

She gave me directions, much more calmly than Jarrod Perkins had. When I turned into the drive, the gates were open. I drove slowly up to the house, figuring there were probably cameras eyeing us; I wanted Perkins to have plenty of time to satisfy himself that I was the Aussie bringing the stuff from Deerdoc to him.

I parked by the front door. There were no other vehicles in evidence. We got out. I didn't even glance at the view. Noticing Ariana's right hand under her jacket, I felt slightly more secure—but not much. If bullets started flying, my TV-viewing told me to drop to the ground. I checked it out. Gravel. It'd be hard on the skin.

"Ariana, the front door's open."

She motioned me to get behind her. "Let me go first."

The hairs on the back of my neck prickled. It was a cliché, but funny how true. "Something's wrong."

Ariana felt it too. She took out her weapon, a sleek automatic. Black, of course. Her body was coiled steel, ready to react to any threat. I think that was the moment I really fell for her.

She pushed at the front door. It swung open. "Mr. Perkins?" I called. "It's Kylie Kendall. I've got the stuff from Deerdoc for you."

Silence. Ariana, not moving her eyes from the hallway in front of us, said, "Is his assistant, Sven, supposed to be here?"

"Perkins never mentioned him. He just said he expected me at ten."

The house was furnished in generic rental style. It had an empty feeling. I didn't know whether to trust my instincts, but I said, too loudly, "Ariana, no one's here."

She signaled to me to be quiet. "Room by room," she said.

The living room was empty. So was the kitchen. We went into the master bedroom together. The bed was made, everything was tidy. I pushed open the door of the adjoining bathroom. "Ariana."

She moved to stand beside me, then grabbed me when I sagged. Jarrod Perkins was sitting in the shower recess, legs splayed, a gun in his lap, his brains blown in a red-and-white pattern across the tiles.

SIXTEEN

Ariana handled the LAPD when the patrol car arrived. Until then I'd wandered around the house, trying to hang on to the contents of my stomach. Ariana had found me in the study, checking out the papers on the desk. "Don't touch anything."

Now I sat quietly to one side while Ariana talked to the two young patrol officers. I'd seen dead bodies before, my grandparents, for example, but their passing had none of the violence of this. Perkins had been a despicable human being, but I felt hollowed by his death.

More cars arrived, more cops conferred with Ariana. It was obvious she knew one bloke personally. Even before the coroner's people had arrived, I heard the cops talking suicide.

We gave brief statements and were about to go when Sven arrived in a huge black vehicle. I peered at it, and Ariana said, "It's a Cadillac SUV."

Sven flung his bulky body out of the SUV and demanded of the nearest cop, "What the fuck's happened?"

"Your name?"

"Sven Larsen. I live here. Personal assistant to Mr. Perkins." He swung his head around, his angry expression fading. "What's wrong? What's happened?"

"Where have you been, sir?"

"The gym. I go every morning. What's going on?"

We left as he was led into the house. Ariana drove, because I was still too shaky. After a long few minutes, I said, "Was it suicide?"

"Hell, no," said Ariana. "Can you really imagine Jarrod Perkins killing himself? Killing someone else, yes. Himself? No."

"Are you saying murder?"

Ariana shot me a hard blue stare. "I'm saying murder."

⊃

I thought of begging off my date with Chantelle, having seen a corpse that morning, but I was looking forward to going somewhere new, with someone I didn't really know. It would be an escape from the indelible picture of the slumped body in the shower recess. I kept myself busy checking through Dad's things in the boxes Ariana had packed up and customizing his computer to suit me. Ariana had gone out, and nobody disturbed me, except for Harriet, who sweetly checked to make sure I was okay then left me alone.

Chantelle had told me to dress casually, so I put on freshly ironed jeans and a blue tunic top. My battered face was a disaster area beyond repair, so I decided to tough it out with dark glasses until the lights in the theater went down.

I explained to Julia Roberts I was going out and might be quite late. She checked that I'd filled her dinner bowl then made it clear she didn't care.

Chantelle was picking me up, and she arrived as Melodie was leaving. "You're Melodie!"

"You're Chantelle!"

I realized they had never met in person, though they'd certainly shared quite intimate information via the receptionist gossip network.

Melodie was appraising Chantelle with approval. "Acting?"

"Amateur stuff mainly. You?"

Melodie assumed a modest expression. "Some. I have a call-back for *Angel Rejects*."

"Angelique?"

"How did you know?"

"You're perfect for the part."

Later, in Chantelle's car, a red Jeep, I said, "I didn't know you were into acting."

"I'm not, really. Practically everyone in this town dreams of being an actor. The rest are aiming to be scriptwriters." She gurgled with laughter. "Sweeping statement, of course, but with a core of truth."

Something was puzzling me. "If you and Melodie have talked so much, how come you didn't know she was"—I was about to say a would-be actor, but Melodie would hate that—"an actor?"

"We don't talk about personal things, we're at *work*."

"But I know for a fact you and Melodie discussed me."

"That's different."

Plainly there were receptionist networking rules I'd never understand.

Sooner or later the subject of Jarrod Perkins had to come up. It was sooner. "You found Jarrod Perkins."

I made an indeterminate, let's-not-discuss-this noise. Didn't work. She repeated the question.

I said, "Yes, it was horrible."

No way was she going to drop the subject. "Shit, Kylie, you saw Perkins yesterday. Right off the wall. Never heard a man scream that way. He said something about blackmail..." She trailed off, sending me a fill-in-the-blanks look.

"Did he?"

"When the news came he'd shot himself, I wasn't surprised. Obviously, he was losing it. Maybe this blackmail thing pushed him over the edge."

"I'd rather not talk about it tonight."

Clearly disappointed, Chantelle said, "Sure." Two minutes later: "Melodie said you were white as a ghost this morning when you came back."

"Thank you, Melodie."

"And she's been fending off reporters all day."

"She has?" This would be the first time Melodie had failed to spill the beans.

"Ariana Creeling told her not to worry you."

Crikey, Ariana had more clout than I'd realized. I hadn't thought anyone or anything could shut Melodie up. And I hadn't thought of Ariana for minutes, and now here she was, popping up again.

"So did you actually see the body?"

"Chantelle!"

She took both hands off the wheel to gesture she was giving up. "Okay, subject's off the menu."

I pushed Ariana out of my mind and concentrated on Chantelle. She was looking spectacular tonight. Her silk shirt was a rich golden yellow and glowed against her dark skin. I felt a tickle of anticipation, but that may have been my stomach. I'd got over the shock of the morning's discovery and was feeling ravenous.

We ate in a little Indian restaurant in the same block as the theater. The place was semi-dark and packed full of noisy patrons. I loved it because it was so full of life, and life was something I found myself valuing more than ever.

The theater was hardly larger than the restaurant. I'd taken off my dark glasses, as I reckoned no one was looking at me anyway. We sat in the front row on a low bench, our knees protruding into the stage area. The play, Chantelle confided, had been written by a friend of hers; it was called *Voices From the Walls.*

I steeled myself, expecting something perplexing and experimental, but it turned out to be a broad farce about the entertainment business. The audience roared with laughter through most of the performance. Being a foreigner, I didn't get all the references, but I enjoyed it all the same.

Afterward we went backstage and crammed into a tiny dressing room to meet the cast and Chantelle's friend, the writer-director. He was a puppy-dog type of bloke, hopeful and ingratiating. If he'd had a tail, he'd have wagged it madly.

A spontaneous party was starting, and suddenly I wanted to get away. Reading my mind, Chantelle murmured, "Let's get out of here. My place?"

I looked into her eyes and felt a sudden jolt of freedom. No one knew me, no one cared what I did. This was someone I didn't really know, and she didn't know me.

"I'm game," I said. "But my nose...you'll be gentle?"

Arms around each other, we laughed our way to her Jeep. I felt giddy, like I was a kid again, on the edge of something new and exciting.

Chantelle had an apartment in West Hollywood just off Santa Monica Boulevard. We made it through the front door before we kissed, quite gently, in the darkness. And then more insistently, until my skin tingled and the core of me began to melt.

Chantelle laughed against my lips. "Do you want to shower with me or go to bed with me?"

"Both, please." My knees were growing weak. "Bed first?"

Everything shook. The floor beneath us creaked, the window shutters rattled. Then it was still again.

"Stone the crows! What was *that*?"

Unconcerned, Chantelle nuzzled my neck. "Probably an aftershock."

"What the hell's an aftershock?"

"From L.A.'s last big earthquake. Aftershocks go on for years. Of course, it could have been a small earthquake in its own right."

I tightened my arms around her. What was it about danger pumping up one's sexual responses? I was living proof it worked. Trembling with both alarm and passion, I said, "Jeez, Chantelle, you're awfully casual about this. I mean, an earthquake!"

Another less violent shaking rolled through the apartment, dancing the shutters again. "Yerks!"

"Calm down. After you live in L.A. for a while, you'll get used to it."

I doubted it, I doubted it strongly. But I was finding Chantelle a delightful antidote to fear. The bed was super-size, the sheets were crisp, her body was lithe and strong, her skin like satin. Her mouth devoured me, her hands traced electric patterns on my willing flesh.

"You're pretty crash-hot," I breathed.

"That's good?"

"That's very good."

I was tight, I was liquid fire, I was flying. Sensations rippled, caught at my heart, exploded.

"Tell me what you want," she whispered.

"I want to fall into the flames."

SEVENTEEN

A bit singed, but happy and rather tired, I made my way home next morning. As it was Saturday, I wasn't expecting anyone except Jules to be there, so it was a surprise to find both Ariana's BMW and Dave Deer's white Rolls in the parking lot.

When I got near Ariana's office I could hear Dave Deer's agitated tones.

"Already I've had cancellations! And these are big names, Ariana, big names! They don't like scandal, they demand complete confidentiality. If it gets out that Perkins was being blackmailed, they'll run for the hills, they'll desert me. And after all I've done for mental health in this town!"

I stuck my head around the door to say I was there, and Ariana beckoned me in.

Dave Deer glanced at me and said, "Your face looks like hell." Then he was back on subject. "Ariana, I'm telling you. Any hint of blackmail is death to Deerdoc. Death!"

"No blackmail letter was found."

"You sure?"

"I spoke with the detective in charge. We go back a long way. I mentioned blackmail, and he said nothing was found."

"Shit! You mentioned blackmail to him? You should have kept that quiet."

"Dave, this is a murder we're talking about."

He stuck out his bottom lip, just like a big baby who'd been scolded. "The news says suicide."

"The LAPD are saying suicide too, because Perkins was shot with his own gun. But every instinct I have says it's not true. Perkins was murdered."

"Then you have to find out who did it. Money's no object here. You've got to do something before my practice disappears down the bloody gurgler."

Ariana indicated the fat envelope we'd taken up to the murder scene and then brought back with us. "The material we had for Perkins. You can take it back with you."

He looked as though she'd offered him a funnel-web spider to play with. "Keep it! I can't afford to have that stuff anywhere in the offices. If they start investigating a murder, there could be search warrants. Keep it here, safe."

When Ariana showed her surprise at the request, he explained, "Only two disks were taken from the file. In that envelope are records of other therapy sessions and my clinical notes. I'll put it this way—Perkins was very frank. There are names, events. If they got out..."

Ariana raised an eyebrow. Her skepticism drove Dave Deer to justify his judgment. "Lorelei Stevens, for example. Perkins caught her in bed with two underage kids, a precocious brother and sister, who happen to be stars themselves."

"Not Tad and Helena Prosser?" Even Ariana seemed startled. I vaguely remembered them as a brother and sister acting team who'd made a series of kid's movies where they played orphans who'd been trained as junior spies.

Dave Deer said bitterly, "They and their pushy mother are patients of mine!" He slapped his forehead with the heel of one hand. "And you wonder why I'm upset!"

166

I said, "But I heard Lorelei Stevens was going to star in the movie Perkins was about to make."

"At half her normal salary," Dave Deer declared. "Now why do you think that was?"

Taking a punt, I said, "In the sessions, did Perkins ever talk about stealing scripts from new writers? I was wondering if he mentioned someone called Rich Westholme."

Dave Deer made a dismissive gesture. "For God's sake," he said, "do you think I *listen* to their self-centered ramblings? Jesus! I'd go mad. Perkins mentioned lots of names. I paid no attention. The only reason I homed in on Lorelei is because she's a patient."

After he'd gone, Ariana and I repaired to the kitchen, Ariana for coffee, me for tea. Spooning grounds into the percolator, she said, "What's your take on this?"

"You mean what do I think? Well, first of all, Jarrod Perkins is the perfect victim. Everyone hated him."

"Agreed."

"I get the impression there's any number of struggling writers who claim he stole material from them."

"Happens all the time, but Perkins had it down to a fine art. For novice writers, the dice are loaded. Perkins, like other successful directors, is the one with the name, the clout, the studios behind him. Who's going to win if there's a dispute?"

She watched me heat the teapot and make sure the kettle was boiling again before pouring the bubbling water over the tea leaves. "Aren't tea bags easier?"

"Oh, please. Do you like instant coffee?"

"Point taken."

I was warming to this discussion. Every now and then I'd think, *This is me, Kylie Kendall, discussing P.I. business.* Like I really knew what the hell I was talking about.

"Sven could have killed him," I said. "I'd reckon Perkins would have been the boss from hell, and maybe Sven finally got totally jack of him. Then there's Randy Romaine." I touched my nose and winced. "I'd love him to be a murderer, though right now I can't think of why he'd bother. And I'm sure Lorelei Stevens would like to see Perkins dead."

"Not necessarily," said Ariana. "For all his faults, he was a very successful director. Lorelei's had a couple of under-performing movies lately. She needs a hit."

While I was digesting this information about the ways of the biz, Ariana said, "Have you considered the possibility that Jarrod Perkins was engineering the whole blackmail plot? He could have used it to extort money from Deerdoc. You know from this morning's conversation that Dave Deer is prepared to pay a great deal to keep his company viable."

I was mortified that I hadn't considered this possibility. But of course, Ariana had been at this a lot longer than me. "What about the bomb in the Hummer?"

"The crime lab's come up with the composition of the device. Pyrotechnics, used in movies."

"The stuff that blows up cars and things?"

"Exactly. And no problem for Perkins to get hold of it."

"What do the police think about the Hummer, now that Perkins is dead?"

"They don't think there's necessarily a connection. There are three theories: one, it was an accident, caused when improperly stored pyrotechnics ignited; two, someone with a grudge against Perkins destroyed the vehicle; three, Jarrod Perkins did it himself."

"Why would he do that?"

She shrugged. "It got attention. You can't buy that type of publicity. And did you notice how he mentioned his movie in every interview?"

Ariana poured her coffee, I poured my tea. We sat down at the bench. I said, "Bob Verritt hates Jarrod Perkins."

Ariana raised her eyebrows. "You're accusing one of our employees of murder?"

My heart took a little jump. One of *our* employees? Was Ariana coming around to the idea I was her partner? In business only, of course.

"Just trying to cover everything," I said demurely. "So how about Dave Deer? He's got a motive."

She nodded approval. "He certainly has—shutting Perkins up before he ruins Deerdoc."

"So what happens if our client turns out to be the murderer? Who pays the bill? Could we sue Deerdoc?"

"You know," said Ariana, "you're one of a kind."

⊃

Last night a play. Tonight an art gallery. Soon I'd be a cultured little Aussie. My second date in as many days. Maybe not a real date, but it would do for the moment. Ariana came back to the office to pick me up at six o'clock. She said to dress up a bit, so I put on my second-best clobber, one of the outfits Harriet had helped me buy for my extremely short career as personal assistant to Dave Deer.

The art gallery where Ariana's sister was exhibiting was in Santa Monica. I'd heard about Santa Monica in songs, and read about it in books, and seen it in movies, but I'd never been there.

When I told Ariana this, she said, "After the gallery, I'll give you a quick tour."

"That'd be bonzer."

The gallery was in a two-story building, and inside it was stark, off-white, echoing rooms with nowhere to sit, except for an odd stone bench here and there. The floor was bare, polished wood. Every wall I could see had widely spaced paintings displayed. A sculpture, looking like a woman with severe deformities, writhed on a pedestal just inside the entrance.

There were lots of people wandering around, some stopping to confer in front of paintings, others snaffling wine and cheese. We'd been there two minutes when we were greeted by a cold-faced woman in a severely cut red suit. She gave a chilly glance at me then recognized Ariana and immediately warmed up. "Ariana, darling!" Air kisses. "I'll tell Janette you're here."

I drifted over to the nearest painting and eyeballed it. It was quite eerie: an almost photographic depiction of a commonplace park with people sitting on benches and kids playing. But nobody had eyes. It was signed in a scrawling *Janette* and the date.

"What do you think?" said Ariana.

"Creepy."

Ariana cocked her head and looked at the painting through narrowed eyes. "Disconcerting," she said. "That's what Janette means to do. Disconcert you."

"Does she only use her first name, like Cher or Madonna?"

"Exactly like Cher or Madonna," said a laughing voice behind us.

Ariana and her sister embraced, then I was introduced. Just seeing her in a crowd, I would have guessed Janette was Ariana's sister. She had the same pale hair and blue eyes, but none of Ariana's taut personality. She was warm, friendly, and down-to-earth, and carrying quite a few kilos more than her sister.

"What do you think of my paintings?" she asked.

"I've only seen one."

"You must let me show you some more."

Some of her work was way past disconcerting—it was straight-out disturbing. One that particularly caught my attention showed a billiard table, meticulously rendered, sitting in a room with a glass wall, outside which was the blue water of a swimming pool. On the green baize of the table lay a human hand, fingers curled, the still-sticky blood indicating it had been freshly removed. And under the table, by one heavy wooden leg, a bare foot with painted nails was similarly amputated.

"Has it got a name?"

"*Hand-Eye Coordination.*"

I frowned at her. "I don't get it."

Janette pointed to the rack holding the cues. I'd missed it at first viewing. Balanced on the top of one cue stick was an eye, newly torn from its socket.

"That's a bit sick," I said.

Janette laughed heartily. "It is, isn't it?"

"Frankly, my mother's certifiable."

"Fran, darling, you deigned to come," said Janette. "And Quip too. My cup runneth over."

"Certifiable and sarcastic," said Fran.

Quip grabbed his mother-in-law's waist and whirled her around, her feet off the floor, until she shrieked for mercy. "You're a *horrible* woman," he declared, releasing her. "When are you going to paint my portrait?"

"When you're famous."

"That'll be *any* day now," Quip declared, his handsome face lit with enthusiasm. He struck a hands-on-hips pose that was so gay I almost applauded. "I've got someone *very* interested in one of my scripts."

"He's gorgeous, Fran," I said to her. Her lips hovered on a smile but never quite made it.

"That's wonderful news." Janette put her arm through his. "We'll have to break out the champagne. Is it anyone I'd know?"

"Probably not. He's an up-and-coming director, been working with Jarrod Perkins. His name's Rich Westholme."

Beside me, Fran grunted. "Asshole," she murmured.

"Fuckwit," I said. We nodded acknowledgment to each other.

I didn't spend any time with Ariana, but I always knew where she was in the gallery. I chatted with various people, smiled cheerfully when the umpteenth one said "I just love your accent" or, for variation, "Australia? I've always wanted to go there, but it's such a long way..."

There were lots of red stickers on paintings, indicating they'd already sold. I wondered where I'd hang a painting of Janette's if I had one. The subject matter would be too weird for a bedroom. In fact, when I thought about it, I couldn't think of anywhere in a house I'd put a painting of hers.

The crowds were thinning, the wine drying up, the few chunks of uneaten cheese looking far from fresh. "Ready to go?" Ariana asked.

"Have you got any of Janette's paintings in your house?" I hadn't seen any in the living room or kitchen, but that didn't mean there weren't rooms crammed with artworks somewhere in the place.

She paused, as though she weren't going to answer, then she said, "One, in my bedroom."

"Your bedroom?" I was startled to think she'd hang one in there.

"It's an early work of Janette's, a watercolor of a mountain lake. Quite beautiful, really. And nothing like any of these."

In the end, we did have a sort of a date. Fran and Quip and Ariana and I went down to the Santa Monica Pier. I'd never seen anything like it. The pier, crowded with people, stretched out into the ocean. Quip said the pier was 2,000 feet long. I asked how much that was in meters. "Like *I'd* know," he said, laughing.

We ate hot dogs, examined the old merry-go-round with its carved wooden horses, rode on the Ferris wheel—I wouldn't risk my life on the roller coaster—and joined the people strolling along to the end of the pier and back again.

I didn't think of Raylene once. Well, maybe once, when I saw two girls wander along with their arms around each other. One of them reminded me of Raylene, I'm not sure why.

Later, when Ariana was driving me home, the fizz of the evening went to my head. I couldn't blame the wine—the gentle buzz from it was long gone—but I'd had such a good time on the pier I felt bold enough to say, "You're an enigma, Ariana."

"I'm not at all."

"Well, of course you'd say you weren't. Otherwise you wouldn't be one." I liked the word, so I said it again. "An enigma."

Silence. Then Ariana said, "You're only saying that because I don't talk about myself."

"Why don't you?"

She glanced across at me, her expression...an enigma. She said, "Why don't *you*?"

I felt a jab of indignation. "Fair crack of the whip! I do. My life's an open book."

"Is it? I don't recall your mentioning anything much about your life in Australia."

Oh, jeez. She had me there. How could I talk about Raylene, and the Wombat's Retreat, and how I'd been elbowed out by Jack, and...

"Forget I brought up the subject."

"Okay."

Wouldn't it rot your socks? This round to Ariana, no worries.

EIGHTEEN

Sunday I went shopping for garden furniture, having decided I'd spring for the cost, since I'd be the one using it. I had a beaut time choosing what to get, finally settling on a round redwood table with a hole in the middle for a shade umbrella, four chairs, and a reclining lounge with dark green all-weather cushions. The umbrella I ordered was dark green too. Delivery, the bloke assured me, would be next week.

I realized this was an awful lot of furniture just for me, but I reckoned I could lure some of the others out there too, once I'd gussied-up the backyard with plants, and maybe a pot or two.

That thought sent me in search of a nursery. It was amazing how many Aussie plants were there. I said so to one of the nursery people, and she said California had a similar climate to Oz, which made a lot of sense. I'd already noticed the gum trees everywhere, and they all seemed to be doing well.

Second-to-last stop was a pet store, where I bought Jules a couple of grooming brushes, a wire comb, and clippers to trim her claws. I felt a bit guilty doing this without asking Melodie if she minded, but it seemed to me Julia Roberts and I were destined to spend the foreseeable future together. Not that I could foresee very far.

Last stop was the supermarket. Hell's bells, the supermarkets in L.A., compared to Wollegudgerie, really were *super*markets. The 'Gudge Mart was a puny little thing compared to the one I was in, which was so vast and had so many choices I almost wished I'd brought a thermos with hot tea so I could have a reviving cuppa halfway through.

When I got home I called Chantelle, told her I'd had a terrific time on Friday, and sort of hinted I might be available for more of the same. Obligingly, she suggested we do something next weekend. My social life was looking up.

Monday morning I went to confess to Ariana I'd ordered garden furniture and to float the bright idea I'd had of putting a washer and a dryer in the storage room next to the kitchen. It'd be child's play, I'd explain, to knock down a wall and make the laundry an alcove to the kitchen. And any plumber could connect the clothes washer to the kitchen drain. Of course, there'd probably have to be an exhaust fan to get rid of the heat from the dryer, but no real probs.

When I knocked on her door I discovered Sven Larsen was there. His Mr. Universe body overwhelmed the chair in which he sat, and I had the thought that it might collapse at any moment.

"Come in, Kylie. Mr. Larsen's here to give his side of the story."

"The cops are stupid," Sven declared. "I know what they're thinking. That I killed Jarrod. Why would I do that, eh? Kill my meal ticket? I'd be a fool."

"The LAPD are saying it appears to be suicide," Ariana said.

"No one who knew Jarrod would believe that. He'd never kill himself, never in a thousand years."

"What's your scenario?"

The chair creaked despairingly as Sven leaned forward, his face intense. He really wanted Ariana to believe him. "Jarrod had a night shoot on Wednesday. A scene that didn't work in the final cut of *Last Train to Hell* and had to be redone. We were up until three a.m., so I knew he'd sleep in. I didn't get breakfast for him like I usually do but went straight to the gym."

He jerked his head in my direction. "He knew she was coming at ten, so he set his alarm for nine-thirty. After I left, someone came in and killed him. Made it look like suicide."

Ariana said, "Did you tell the detectives your theory?"

Sven scowled. "It's not a theory, lady! It's what happened. And yes, I told them. They said they were following every lead." He gave a derisive grunt. "Every lead? I don't think so."

"When you last saw Mr. Perkins, what sort of mood was he in?"

Sven smiled sourly. "He was like always, only louder. He chewed me out in front of the crew on the shoot."

"Chewed you out, how?"

"He fired me. But he was always doing that. I paid no mind to it. And it wasn't me he was mad at, it was Deer. He said he'd tear his balls off and push them down his throat. Blamed him for the whole blackmail thing."

Feeling left out, I said, "Did you see the blackmail letter?"

Sven gave me an irritated glance. "He told me about it. Half a million. For that he'd get the recordings back."

"Would Mr. Perkins have paid?" Ariana asked.

Sven laughed harshly. "You kidding me? Jarrod was a mean motherfucker. He wouldn't pay a cent."

I said, "Was anything missing from the house?"

Sven swung his heavy head around. "What?"

"Was anything missing?"

He frowned. "Only scripts. Jarrod always had his desk piled with movie scripts. But they were gone. I figured the police..."

He heaved himself to his feet. The chair seemed relieved. "I know you're working for Deer. I wanted you to hear my side of the story." His face contorted with anger. "Fucking cops. Once they think it's murder, it'll be me. Easy target. Dumb body-builder. They won't look any further."

There was something almost pathetic about Sven as he leaned forward earnestly and said to Ariana, "I didn't do it. Please believe me."

After he'd gone, Ariana said, "I'd hate to think he's right, but if murder's on the table, Sven Larsen's the easy target, with opportunity and motive. Why look any further?"

"Why would anyone take scripts?" I asked. "What would be the point?"

Ariana looked thoughtful. "That's a good question."

We discussed it for a few minutes, then I changed the subject. "I've ordered some garden furniture. I'm paying."

"Fine." She tilted her head. "I've got a feeling there's something more."

"I do have this idea..."

Wary, Ariana said, "Yes?"

I explained my vision of a laundry room. Ariana listened without comment. When I ran out of steam, she said, "So you've given up on the idea of an apartment? You're going to stay here instead?"

"In the short term, yes."

"And in the long term?"

"Do you still want to get rid of me?"

Ariana blinked. "Is that what you think?"

"I know you wanted me to get lost that first day, and probably the second and the third." I grinned. "Hell, that whole first week."

"I admit it was a surprise to have you arrive out of the blue."

"I know you wanted to freeze me out. But lately you've stopped. Why is that?"

"Exhaustion," said Ariana.

Ɔ

I was sending a bunch of postcards back to Oz to assure friends I hadn't been mugged or carjacked yet. I took them to the front desk, where there was a basket for outgoing mail. Melodie took a call, then said to me with open curiosity, "Dr. Deer's wife is on the line for you." She shoved the receiver at me. "You can take it here."

I chatted with Elise for a few minutes, then handed the phone back to Melodie. She looked at me so expectantly, I grinned. "You're dying to know what that was about, aren't you?"

"I sure am."

"Elise wants to take me to some spa place today. She's says it's a gift from her for putting myself on the line at Deerdoc."

"No! Which one?"

"I think she called it Pampering Hands."

"Pampering Hands?" Melodie looked at me with something approaching awe. "They've got a real exclusive clientele. You know who goes there? Cameron Diaz, and George Clooney, and Oprah Winfrey when she's in town..." She shook her head in wonderment. "You have all the luck, Kylie. You've barely hit the ground, and you're going to Pampering Hands!"

I left her calling the receptionist hotline.

"What am I letting myself in for?" I asked Elise. "I've never been to one of these spa places. You'd better tell me what to expect."

She flashed me a smile. "I'd like it to be a complete surprise."

"I'm not too sure I'm ready for it."

"Trust me," she said. She ran a light and turned left to a chorus of horns. "I just know you're going to love Pampering Hands. When I'm tense and tired, there's nothing better. I try to go at least once a week."

We glided down Rodeo Drive, Elise's blood-red Rolls Royce convertible getting plenty of stares. She patted the pale cream leather of her seat. "Birthday present from Dave. Sensational car, isn't it?"

I smiled at her, warmed by her unaffected pleasure in luxury. "Terrif," I said, "but I'd worry every time I parked, in case someone scratched it."

Elise gave a airy wave. "When I'm out I never park the thing myself. There's always valet."

The proof of this statement was demonstrated when we drew up at the curb in front of a gorgeous little building made to look like a miniature Greek temple. Almost before we'd stopped, two blokes wearing black jumpsuits with the words PAMPERING HANDS SPA on their chests had our doors open.

"Ms. Deer! Welcome to Pampering Hands!"

We were met at the door by a slim young woman wearing a white tunic and sandals. "Ms. Deer! How wonderful to see you again."

She turned her smile on me. It wavered for a moment when she saw my black eye, which was now an interesting shade of khaki, and my still-swollen nose. Even so, I thought she might still say it was wonderful to see me too, but she didn't. "And your guest...?"

"G'day. Call me Kylie," I said.

"What a lovely name."

"It's Aboriginal for boomerang."

The woman seemed a bit thrown by this. "How fascinating."

She glided off toward a big stone altar affair and consulted a screen set into its surface. "Ah!" she exclaimed with professional delight. "Ms. Deer, I see you've chosen for yourself our ultra-detoxifying mud wrap, followed by a Ayurvedic Shirodhara. And for your friend..."

"Kylie," I said.

"And for Kylie you've chosen a salt exfoliation, followed by the Pampering Hands full-body massage. An excellent regimen for one's first visit to our wonderful spa. And then, of course, both of you will complete your pampering with a relaxing Pampering Hands mineral salts spa bath."

As she led us down a white marble corridor, I said to Elise, "I can make a stab at what a mud wrap might be, but what's the thing you're having after it?"

Overhearing me, the young woman said in reverent tones, "Ayurvedic Shirodhara is a wonderful, ancient East Indian ritual. Warm sesame oil is poured over the third eye in one's forehead, followed by an Indian head massage. We highly recommend it, to release blocked energy and to clear the mind."

"Sounds wonderful," I said, with just a touch of mockery.

She gave me a patronizing smile. "Would you like me to explain your salt exfoliation and full-body massage?"

"Please don't. Let's leave it as a wonderful surprise."

I was left alone in a candlelit room, furnished with a massage table. I felt its surface and found it was heated. Beside was a chrome bench covered with a multitude of exotically shaped bottles containing lotions and oils. I discovered they were warmed too. My skin prickled: Someone was watching me.

A short, tunic-clad woman with alarmingly muscled arms had soft-footed it into the room. "I'm Veeda," she hissed, peering at me with an evaluating stare. "Your first time here at Pampering Hands Spa?"

"Too right."

"Please disrobe completely."

"What? Everything?"

"Everything."

I met up with Elise again in the mineral salts spa bath. "Phew," I said, slipping into the bubbling water beside her. "I'm exfoliated and massaged to the billy-oh. There isn't a bit of me that hasn't been pounded and squeezed."

"You didn't absolutely love every moment?" She seemed astonished.

"I'm not used to total strangers getting quite that intimate with my body," I said.

"Who was your masseuse?"

"Veeda."

"Oh, *Veeda*. I've had her." Elise chuckled. "She has a particularly vigorous approach and a firm touch."

"Crikey, she sure does."

"But don't you feel relaxed?" Elise asked. "Renewed?"

I wriggled my shoulders. "You know," I said, "I think I do."

Elise discussed the spa for a few moments, stopped to point out she was sure she'd seen Barbara Walters in the adjacent massage room, then said, mega-casually, "How's the investigation going?"

"Investigation?"

"Oh, come on, Kylie. Don't play dumb with me. You know what I'm talking about. The whole Jarrod Perkins thing."

"Didn't Dave tell you all about it? He hired us."

Elise frowned heavily. "Dave won't discuss the matter. He's suddenly developed the old-fashioned idea that his wife should be protected from harsh reality."

"What harsh reality?"

"That's what I'd like to know," said Elise. "Frankly, I'm worried Dave is hiding something from me."

Feeling like a real detective, I weighed up what searching question I should ask. The best I could come up with was, "Do you think he had something to do with the murder?"

This amused Elise. "Dave kill someone? He hasn't got the guts. And even if he did, I could handle it. It's something a lot more serious."

More serious than murder? "What is it?" I asked.

"The most important thing in the world. Money. Think what the publicity could do to Deerdoc if the murder investigation gets too close."

"I thought any publicity was good publicity."

Elise made a face. "Not with Dave's clients." She dropped her voice so low I could hardly hear her above the bubbling water. "I'm not expecting you to break confidences, but one Aussie to another, I'm asking you to warn me if the shit's going to hit the fan in a big way. I want to get out with my finances intact, no matter what happens to Dave. Know what I mean?"

I knew what she meant.

NINETEEN

I spent the rest of the week working on my private eye skills. Harriet and Lonnie gave me preliminary lessons on using public records to background individuals, and showed me how to trace people who had skipped to avoid debt or responsibilities like child care payments.

This exercise got a bit more interesting when Randy Romaine skipped bail and disappeared.

Bob took me out in his car and demonstrated moving surveillance. It was fun learning how to follow someone without being noticed. Then I practiced on unsuspecting motorists. Mostly the techniques were common sense, like putting several cars between you and the subject, and driving by then doubling back if the subject turns into a service station. Some things, though, I'd never thought of before.

One was, Bob said with a wink, illegal. This was to get at the subject's vehicle when it was parked. Using a pen or screwdriver, a small hole was punched in one of the plastic brake light covers. This made the car much easier to follow, even in heavy traffic, as every time the driver braked a bright white spot of light blinked on.

I didn't see much of Ariana. She had a deposition in Nevada and then a court appearance in Santa Barbara.

Ɔ

My Aunt Millie called me on Wednesday. As soon as I heard her tart voice I could visualize her sharp-featured face. Aunt Millie was a vinegary soul with an unerring ability to find the negative in every situation.

I'd hardly managed hello before she started. "Kylie Kendall, you're trouble, pure and simple. I said it from the time you were born—that girl's trouble, I said."

"And how are you, Aunt Millie?"

"Not good, but a lot better than your mum."

I felt a thrill of alarm. "What's wrong with Mum?"

"You've broken her heart."

Relieved, I said, "Oh, is that all?"

"Is that all?" she repeated sarcastically. "Typical! Just take a look at your attitude, my girl."

"Aunt Millie—"

"I'd have thought you'd have had some consideration for your family before you went gallivanting over to the States. But no." She paused for me to absorb this. "You always were a head-strong, self-absorbed girl. Even as a child, I knew you'd bring heartbreak to your mother."

"Mum put you up to this, didn't she?"

"I don't know what you mean," said Aunt Millie indignantly.

"Then why are you calling me?"

"Isn't it obvious? You're needed back here at the Wombat's Retreat. Your poor mother is barely coping."

"What about Jack?"

"He's a man," said Aunt Millie. "He does his best, but well..."

Ɔ

Lonnie's birthday was on Saturday, and I was touched to be included in his birthday celebration, which was to be lunch at a restaurant of Lonnie's choice.

"Would you believe," said Melodie on Friday, "Lonnie's gone and picked Shel 'n' Hymie's *again*? He's got no imagination."

"What's wrong with the place?" I asked.

"It's a deli. You don't have a birthday lunch at a deli, 'specially when Kendall & Creeling is picking up the tab."

"Are you talking about a delicatessen? A shop where they sell ham and cheese?"

"No, a New York deli. You know, like Nate 'n' Al's or Jerry's." She gave a discontented sigh. "Why couldn't Lonnie choose one of them? The stars go there."

Shel 'n' Hymie's Deli was in Studio City on Ventura Boulevard. Harriet volunteered to pick me up from Kendall & Creeling so I wouldn't have to find the place myself. We parked across the road in a supermarket lot, meeting up with Lonnie as we walked to the traffic lights. He beamed when we both wished him a happy birthday. "It's so great of you guys to come," he said.

On the other side of the road a faded sign on a nondescript building announced SHEL 'N' HYMIE'S DELI. A metal railing enclosed a few tables in the front, each bolted to the ground and with a grubby yellow umbrella. Traffic thundered past, perfuming the air with exhaust fumes. I couldn't imagine why anyone would sit out there, but most of the tables were occupied.

As we waited for the lights to change, Lonnie said approvingly, "Shel 'n' Hymie's is just like a genuine New York deli. They got it right—the ambiance, the in-your-face style."

"And the great food," said Harriet. "Don't forget the food."

The traffic ground to a halt, one huge truck hissing its airbrakes with irritation. We skipped across the road and through the utilitarian glass door. The ambiance Lonnie admired was provided by the cramped booths lining two sides and the Formica-topped tables filling the rest of the space. The floor was industrial gray, the walls a yucky shade of green. The place was crowded with people talking loudly, sometimes to their companions but frequently into cell phones.

Lonnie was obviously a regular customer. He asked Joyce, a tough-looking bottle-blond wearing a red checkered uniform and white apron, how she was today.

"The usual," she snapped. "I'd complain, but what would be the use?"

She marched us to a corner booth with a view of the traffic outside. It would just be big enough to squeeze in six people. Fran, glaring at a large, laminated menu, was already there. "Bob's going to be late," she said, looking up, "and Melodie is never on time, as we all know."

"Is Ariana coming?" I asked, aware that I'd be terribly disappointed if she wasn't.

Fran shrugged. "Last I heard, she was."

"You expecting more?" demanded an angular woman with a nasal twang. She was wearing the same uniform as Joyce and the same hard expression. The badge on her chest identified her as Dora.

"Three more on their way," said Lonnie. He beamed at her like a cheerful puppy. "Today's my birthday, Dora."

"Many happies," she said, without a change to her dour expression. She slapped menus down in front of us. "Something to drink?"

"Diet Coke," said Fran.

"The same," said Lonnie and Harriet in chorus.

Dora switched her gimlet gaze to me. "You?"

"May I have Coke Coke, please?" I asked. "The real stuff, I mean."

"Three diets and one regular." She spun on her heel and walked off.

"See what I mean about style?" said Lonnie appreciatively. "Dora's got that New York attitude."

"Abrupt, you mean?" I said.

"Rude," said Harriet. "They pride themselves on it."

I scanned the menu as the others chatted. The choice was huge: pastrami, corned beef sandwiches, cheese blintzes, potato pancakes, lox and scrambled eggs... I wasn't sure what half of them were, so I decided to play it safe and order something simple like a corned beef sandwich.

"Before Bob gets here," said Lonnie in a conspiratorial tone, "I have to tell you the cops interviewed him last night. About Jarrod Perkins."

"How do you know that?" asked Fran.

"Because," said Lonnie, "they interviewed me too." He added in a pleased tone, "I told them everything I knew about Reece Quinn."

Harriet looked disgusted. "That is such old news. I can't believe it's come up now."

"Who's Reece Quinn?" I asked.

"Bob's big chance to make the big time." Fran's tone was caustic.

"A couple of years ago," said Harriet, "Perkins claimed he was being stalked, and Bob was hired to assess security at his house. And, like every second person in this town, Bob had an idea for a movie and didn't want to miss this opportunity to offer it to a director."

"Dumb move," said Fran.

Lonnie took up the story. "Bob had a draft script based on his experiences as a P.I. He called the character Reece Quinn."

I could see where this was going. "Jarrod Perkins stole the script?"

"Perkins strung Bob along for a while," said Harriet, "getting his hopes up. Bob spent a lot of time polishing the script. After about six months Perkins lost interest, and the whole thing lapsed."

"Imagine Bob's surprise," said Fran, "when the word leaked out that Jarrod Perkins had a big-time scriptwriter working on an original idea Perkins had come up with. By sheer coincidence, the character and plot points were just like Bob's Reece Quinn script."

"So what happened?"

"Bob had it out with Perkins, but it didn't get him anywhere. There's no copyright on ideas, and Perkins told him to get lost."

I caught sight of Bob Verritt's tall, lanky form through the window. "Here he comes," I said.

Bob slid into the booth beside me. I looked at him sideways, wondering what he'd told the police. He'd just moved up higher on my mental list of suspects, although I couldn't imagine Bob killing anyone, not even Jarrod Perkins.

At that point Melodie arrived in a cloud of explanations of how she'd just had to stop at a couple of sales on the way. "Would you believe," she cried, bundling herself and several shopping bags into the booth, "I got a pair of Manolo Blahnik for half price! Just like the ones Sarah Jessica Parker wore to the awards the other night."

"How much?" Fran asked.

"Three hundred. Marked down from five." Melodie dove into one of the bags and came up with a pair of black stilettos with very high heels.

"Crikey," I said, "people pay that much for shoes?"

"Kylie, they're *Manolo Blahnik*," said Melodie. "I mean, Madonna wears them."

Dora appeared with our drinks. "Three diet. One regular." She slapped them down, then glowered at Melodie and Bob. "Drinks?"

Melodie responded with—no surprise—"Diet Coke, please." Bob asked for iced tea. Dora grunted and departed.

"Dora's not all that happy in her work," I said.

"Nonsense," said Lonnie. "I know for a fact she loves being here at Shel 'n' Hymie's."

Bob grinned. "She told you that?"

"Perhaps not in those words," said Lonnie. "But Dora's been here for years. She wouldn't stay if she didn't love the place."

My pulse gave a little jump when I looked up to see Ariana approaching. Black jeans, black shirt, with a glint of gold at her throat. Wow.

"Happy birthday, Lonnie," she said, handing him an envelope. I'd learned it was office policy to have everyone put in for a present. Lonnie had wanted some obscure bit of electronic equipment and was getting a check so he could buy it himself.

Ariana slid into the booth, Dora materialized, and we all ordered. When our meals came I blinked at the size of my corned beef sandwich. Huge slices of bread, enough corned beef to choke a horse, salad, coleslaw, and pickles. I could stretch this serving to two meals—maybe three.

Joyce herself brought the birthday cake that had been specially ordered. We all sang "Happy Birthday," more or less in tune. Lonnie blushed with pleasure. "Oh, you guys!"

Dora appeared. "Cawfee?" she asked in her grating voice. She stood with one hand on her hip, daring anyone to order.

"Cappuccino, please," I said.

Dora looked at me as if I had crawled out from under a rock. Fran smirked.

Perhaps it was my Aussie accent. I tried again. "Cappuccino?"

"Cappuccino," said Dora with scorn. "Cappuccino? We serve cawfee here. *Cawfee.*"

"Oh," I said, "then in that case, I'll have coffee, please."

Lonnie shook his head as Dora stomped off. "You've gotta love them," he said, "those New York waitresses."

⊃

On Sunday Raylene called. My stomach turned a somersault at the sound of her voice. "Kylie? Your mum gave me your number."

I couldn't think of anything to say.

"Kylie?"

"I didn't expect to hear from you."

"I'm so sorry I hurt you."

I was furious to feel tears sting my eyes. "It's a bit late for that, Raylene."

"I want you to know, I know I made a big mistake."

I shrugged, although of course she couldn't see me.

"Come on, sweetheart," said Raylene, her voice soft, "don't make me beg. I shouldn't have done what I did. I was wrong. I should never have thrown you over for Maria. Please forgive me." She waited for a moment, then said, "Kylie?"

I'd been longing to hear these words. I'd dreamed of her saying them. Now they seemed strangely flat. "It's too late," I said.

"What do you mean? Do you want me to crawl? I'll do it. I was stupid and thoughtless."

"What does Maria think of this turnabout?"

"Don't worry about Maria. She's okay."

"Mum told me you and Maria were planning to go to Bangkok."

"Is that what's upsetting you?" Raylene said. "We can plan a trip together after you get back."

Part of me still loved her, but I knew I'd never trust her again. "I'm not coming back."

"You don't mean that, Kylie. You're just angry with me, and so you should be. I've told you I'm sorry."

I'm sorry too," I said, "but it's over."

"I don't believe you."

I felt an awful sadness run through me. "Raylene, why did you do it?"

"I don't know." She sounded genuinely puzzled. She sighed. "I want it back like it used to be. You and me, together."

"It's gone," I said, and because I didn't want her to hear me crying, I hung up the phone.

Julia Roberts watched me sob, her ears angled in the equivalent of a feline frown. Then she came over and let me hug her, without protesting too much. "You're all I've got, Jules," I said.

She didn't look impressed.

TWENTY

I had a miserable Sunday night, reliving the conversation with Raylene and thinking of all we'd meant to each other. Scenes from our life together kept popping into my mind.

Twice I picked up the phone to call her back, but I didn't. It *was* over. Although I missed her so much, I knew we could never recapture the feelings we'd had for each other.

It was a relief to wake up on Monday morning and hear Luis vacuuming the hallway outside my door. I jumped out of bed full of resolution. It was time to take my Wombat Strategy seriously. I would set my goal and plow my way through any obstacle that got in the way. I'd throw myself wholeheartedly into the P.I. business. Maybe solve Jarrod Perkins's murder. That would take my mind off my troubles.

When Bob Verritt came in I trotted after him into his office. "Bob, can I ask you a question?"

"That depends what it is."

"Lonnie said the police interviewed you about Jarrod Perkins and the Reece Quinn script."

Bob folded his length into his chair and leaned back to give me a thoughtful look. "You can't run before you can walk," he observed.

That sounded like something my mother would say. "I'm fine-tuning my questioning techniques," I said.

Bob grinned at me. "You've got a lot of work to do."

"About Jarrod Perkins..."

"Alibi," said Bob. "I've got an alibi. It checks out, so you can cross me off your list."

I left him chuckling to himself.

Outside, Fran was waiting for me. She took me into my office, closed the door, and said, "What do you know about Rich Westholme?"

"Nothing much. He's a director, or that's what he claims to be. Why?"

Her frown was even darker than usual. "He's been promising Quip too much, for no reason I can see. And I think it's to get to me."

I looked at her, astonished. "He's putting the hard word on you? Of all people, Fran, you should be able to deal with someone like Rich Westholme."

She shook her head impatiently. "No, it's not *that*. Of course I'd rip his balls off. What he's doing is sniffing around anything to do with Jarrod Perkins. I don't know what he's after, but I don't like it."

"Did you say anything to him?"

Fran rolled her eyes. "Quip doesn't want me to upset Westholme, because he thinks he's going to be his meal ticket to the big time."

She glared at me as though somehow all this was my fault. "Now you know."

"What do you want me to do about it?"

Her wicked smile flashed on for a moment. "You're the P.I. I'll leave it all to you."

I decided to front Melodie about Rich Westholme, but she brought up the subject herself. "Kylie, I'm not convinced Rich is really supportive of my career." She jutted her jaw resolutely.

"We're going out tonight, and I'm going to have it out with him."

I sat on the edge of the reception desk and put on a sympathetic, interested expression. "Why do you say he isn't supportive?"

"He told me that first weekend that I'd have a part in *Primal Appetites.*"

"You're talking about a movie? Or was that the menu for the weekend?"

Melodie gave her tinkling laugh. "That's so funny." Then her face grew stern. "This is so tragic. My chance to be in a movie with Jarrod Perkins attached. Like, how often does that happen?"

I clicked my tongue in empathy. "That's awful for you. But how was Perkins involved, exactly?"

"Rich told me Jarrod Perkins just loved his *Primal* script. Said it needed some work but that he was willing to put his name behind it. To produce it while Rich directed!" She sighed dolefully. "Then something went wrong."

"What happened?"

"I'm not sure, but I know Rich is very, very angry. He said he hadn't trusted Perkins from the beginning. That he'd had insurance that Perkins couldn't back out of the deal."

"What did that mean?"

"I don't know. When I asked, he yelled at me."

"I'd dump him," I said.

Melodie was appalled. "Kylie! He's a *director.*"

Thinking of my conversation with Fran, I said, "Has Rich been asking questions about anything in particular?"

A shadow of guilt crossed Melodie's face. "Maybe he has."

"About Jarrod Perkins?"

"I didn't see the harm in telling him we were keeping some stuff here."

"You mean the therapy sessions from Deerdoc."

She bit her lip and nodded. "Don't tell Ariana, will you? She's very strict about things like that." She wriggled her shoulders. "Anyway, what does it matter if Rich knows? He had a lot to do with Perkins. Why wouldn't he be interested?"

I went away and thought about it, then just as Melodie was collecting her things I came back to the reception desk. She gave me a sunny smile. "I'm leaving early tonight, okay?"

Slapping down a fat manila envelope I'd sealed with multiple strips of packing tape, I said with authority, "I think it's better if we send those records back to Deerdoc."

I hadn't checked with Ariana, but she giving a deposition in San Francisco and I'd rationalized it was better not to disturb her.

Melodie stared at the envelope, fascinated. "Is that what we were talking about before?"

"Jarrod's therapy sessions." We both looked at the envelope as though Perkins might materialize and hover over it. I thought it unlikely, though, since the envelope contained blank computer disks and sheets of paper. The real material was secure in Kendall & Creeling's safe.

"It's a bit late for a pickup," said Melodie, checking her watch. What she really meant was she was keen to get out of there.

"Tomorrow morning's fine. There's no real hurry."

I knew, as sure as my name was Kylie Kendall, that Melodie would not be able to resist telling Rich Westholme about the envelope. I was betting that tomorrow morning Rich would make some excuse to turn up here early. He would see it as his only chance to get those disks.

And why? Because according to my theory, the insurance Rich had said he had was blackmail. He'd paid Randy Romaine to get the material on Perkins from the Deerdoc files. And now he'd probably paid Randy to go into hiding.

Ariana was coming home tonight. I'd call her later and tell

her what I'd done. Then she could be here when Rich Westholme incriminated himself.

But by the time everyone had gone and I'd checked that the building was secure, I'd had second thoughts about my plan, which had seemed so smart that afternoon. Imagining myself telling Ariana about it, I blushed. She'd say, "What does it prove if he does go for the envelope?" She'd be right. Rich could talk his way out of it easily.

I was out of my depth here. Training for a few days wasn't enough to make me a P.I.'s bootlace. Disgusted with myself, I retrieved the envelope, emptied out the contents, tore it up, and put the pieces in the nearest wastepaper basket.

I'd have to come clean with Ariana. I'd tell her tomorrow, and she'd laugh at me.

"I'm a total fuckwit," I said to Julia Roberts. She just blinked.

TWENTY-ONE

Embarrassment made me thirsty, so I made a pot of tea. While waiting the four minutes it took to get strong enough, I selected Julia Roberts's dinner. Tonight I was serving chicken. I hoped she'd approve. The illustration on the can made it look quite delicious.

Suddenly I sensed someone was looking at me. Rich Westholme stood in the doorway to the kitchen.

I jumped. "Jeez! You gave me a fright." I looked past him without much hope and said, "Is Melodie with you?"

This couldn't be good. He must have let himself in with Melodie's keys. The way Rich stood, balanced on the balls of his feet, was menacing enough to set my heart racing.

"Would you like a cup of tea? I've just made it."

He didn't bother answering. "Melodie tells me you've been asking questions about my work." He narrowed his eyes. "A lot of pushy questions."

"*Primal Appetites*," I said.

He glared at me. "My script. What of it?"

"Melodie said you were developing it with Jarrod Perkins. That the agreement was he'd produce and you'd direct. She was thrilled because you told her she'd have a part. But it never happened."

"That stupid bitch." I thought how she'd hate to hear the scorn in his voice. "Christ, I'm so sick of hearing her chatter on about her fucking career."

"The latest project Perkins was developing is called *Primitive Obsessions*." I sounded quite calm, though inside I wasn't. "He mentioned it in every interview he gave after his Hummer exploded."

"So?"

"So *Primal Appetites* and *Primitive Obsessions* are awfully similar. I'm thinking maybe they're the same script with different names."

"You're a stupid bitch, like Melodie. You can't keep your mouth shut."

Right now I was tending to agree. What did I think I was doing, needling him like this? I'd persuade him to leave, then call Ariana, the cops, pizza delivery, anyone who'd come.

"Look, Rich," I said reasonably, "it's been nice chatting with you, but I think you should go."

His smile wasn't reassuring. "Do you? You think I should go?"

"Well, yes. You obviously don't have a high opinion of me, so why spend more time in my company than necessary?"

"I'm here to collect something. An envelope."

"If you come back tomorrow, I'm sure someone can find it for you."

He shoved me hard against the counter. "Shut up."

The physical confrontation with Randy Romaine had taught me the disadvantages of being without a weapon. I scanned the counter but saw nothing promising. I'd keep him talking, maybe get him off guard so I could make a run for it. "I saw the Hummer after it was blown up. Perkins was totally spaz."

"Was what?"

"He lost it completely. He was raving mad." Rich's momentary look of satisfaction encouraged me to add, "You planted the bomb, didn't you? Pyrotechnics from a film set?"

"Smart little bitch, aren't you?"

Shaking my head with fake admiration, I said, "You were taking a hell of a chance."

He shrugged. "If you look like you know what you're doing, nobody pays any attention. Perkins never locked the Hummer. I just opened the door. I was fifty yards away before it blew."

"Why bother?"

Rich laughed. "To put the motherfucker on edge," he said, "so he'd roll over when I upped the ante."

Julia Roberts came into the kitchen; it was her dinner time. It was quite unfair. I knew Rich abhorred cats, but she was totally minding her own business when Rich saw her. An expression of deep loathing crossed his face. He aimed a kick that connected with her ribs. Jules did a sort of somersault and landed on her feet, hissing.

"Get outta here!"

Julia got.

That was the final straw. Julia Roberts did not deserve this treatment. I fair dinkum looked for a weapon this time. Something substantial enough to wipe the smirk off this bastard's face. The TV set? Too heavy. There were knives in the drawer, if I could get to them. And cans in the cupboard. Kitchen cleaners under the sink...

"Bitch! Answer me!"

"What?"

"I'm asking you once more, and that's it. The recordings of the sessions Perkins had with that quack, Deer—where are they? Melodie said they were in an envelope at the front desk, waiting to be picked up by UPS. There's nothing there."

I spread my hands. "Can't help you."

He reached into the pocket of his jeans. The flick knife made an obscene little click as it sprang open. "Wrong answer."

My gaze was drawn magnetically to the gleaming blade. Rich jabbed at my face. I recoiled. He laughed.

"Get the hell out of here!" I yelled, not having much hope that he would.

"The envelope."

I shrugged. He moved like a striking snake. Blood sprang from my left breast where he'd pricked me, spreading a bright red stain on my white T-shirt. It wasn't deep, but it stung like hell.

"Fair crack of the whip," I said. "It was only last week I got a black eye and a bloody nose. Now you're stabbing me?" I heard the tremor in my voice.

So did he. "Gee, Kylie," he said mockingly, "am I scaring you?"

I was backed up against the counter. Jammed against me was one of the kitchen stools. I slid my right hand behind me and tried to get a good grip on it. To distract him, I said, "During his therapy, Jarrod Perkins said something about stealing your movie concept, didn't he? Probably discussed how you'd threatened him."

"Smart little cunt, aren't you?" I shrank back as he took a step closer to me. "Last chance," he said. "Where's the envelope?"

"Rich, think this through. If you stop now, it isn't too serious. If you really hurt me, you're in big trouble."

Rich chuckled—not a nice sound. "Sweetheart," he said, "I've done two. Three won't make any difference."

"Randy Romaine's dead?"

"Romaine was a disaster from the get-go. I paid him to take disks of Perkins's sessions, but he got creative and took some of Bart Toller's too. Then the bastard thought he'd go into business for himself, so he swiped Lorelei Stevens's file. He was getting to be a real liability, and he knew far too much about me." I ducked as Rich again jabbed at my face. "Like you," he said.

"And you killed Jarrod Perkins?"

"You want the details?" He showed his teeth in a smile that gave me the willies. This bloke was having fun.

I nodded.

"It wasn't difficult. I waited until his assistant left, then walked in on Perkins getting dressed. I gave him one last chance to cut me into the deal he had for *Primitive Obsessions*. I was more than generous, since it was *my* story and *my* script. The prick laughed at me. So I mentioned the disks and told him I was also asking for a substantial up-front payment. He told me to go to hell and lunged for the gun he kept in his bedside table. No trouble to take it from him."

I tightened my grip on the stool. I'd only have one chance...

"It was fun," said Rich, "watching him beg for his life. He didn't think I had the guts to go through with it. Like you, he thought he'd play along and get away with it."

"And afterward you swiped all the scripts that were on his desk."

"Of course. If the cops didn't buy his death as suicide, then the missing scripts would throw suspicion on all the poor suckers he's recently stolen script ideas from."

Rich made a wide, graceful arc with the knife, slashing across the top of my other breast. I gasped and looked down at the line of red, which widened as I stared. "Such a pity," he said. "Some sexual deviant breaks in and hacks you to pieces. No one will be all that surprised. Bad things happen all the time in this town."

I like to think Julia Roberts came back into the kitchen to help me, although I have to admit her primary purpose may have been her dinner. Whatever Julia's motive, her timing was excellent. I had a firm one-handed grip on the kitchen stool behind me. When Rich, seeing the cat, made a sound of disgust and went to deliver a second kick, two things happened: Julia Roberts skipped out of the way with great agility, clearly having learned from experience, and I swung the kitchen stool at Rich's head as hard as I could.

When it connected there was a satisfying *thwack*! Rich went down on one knee. Then he was up again, swearing, his knife flashing like a deadly extension of his hand. I took another swing, but he deflected it with an upraised arm then wrenched the stool from me.

Blood was pouring down his face. "I'll kill you, you fucking bitch."

He was staggering, dazed but still terribly dangerous. He slashed at me and I leapt backward to avoid the blade. If I could make the door and escape...but he was blocking the way.

I made a silent apology to Fran, picked up my prized pottery teapot with both hands, and brought it down on his head.

The teapot shattered. Rich fell with a crash to the floor at my feet, lying motionless in a pool of tea and tea leaves.

TWENTY-TWO

The police, sirens wailing, arrived the same time as the para-medics. Then Ariana. Then Bob Verritt. Then Harriet.

I'd been perfectly calm up until then, but this was like my family arriving to support me. This thought made me sniffle a bit, but fortunately no one knew why.

I blew my nose and answered the cops' questions as best I could, until I was drooping with the combination of shock and lack of food. That reminded me of poor Julia Roberts, who had never got her chicken dinner. Bob grinned at me and said he'd take care of it.

Rich had been carried out on a stretcher, alive and swearing and accompanied by a cop.

While Ariana and Bob dealt with the situation, Harriet took me to the nearest emergency hospital, where we waited for hours until a harried young doctor had time to dress my wounds.

It was daylight by the time Harriet drove me back. Ariana was the only one there. "I'll look after her," she said to Harriet. "You go on home."

"I'm fine," I said, once we were inside. "I'm starving, though. Lunch was the last meal I ate."

"I'll scramble you some eggs. Can you face being in the kitchen?"

"No worries." Even so, I peered around the door before I entered. I thought there might be police tape, but everything had been cleaned up. There was no blood on the floor, no tea or shards of pottery. I looked mournfully at the spot on the counter where I'd kept my teapot.

"Fran will buy you a new one," said Ariana.

"It won't be as good," I said. "They never are."

She was smiling when the building shuddered. "Whoa," she said. "Earthquake. Get in the doorway. It's the safest place."

Oh, jeez! This was much worse than the tremors I'd felt at Chantelle's. It was as if some gigantic animal had the building in its jaws and was shaking it violently.

It was almost impossible to stand. Ariana and I clung together while the ground bucked and groaned and rolled beneath our feet.

The sounds of the earth tearing itself apart faded, and the shaking stopped. I was suddenly conscious of Ariana's arms around me. Of mine around her. Our first embrace? Maybe our last. The shaking was beginning again.

"Oh, no," I said. "One's enough."

Rending sounds, a deep roar bursting from the depths. The earth in pain. I looked into Ariana's blue, blue eyes. "Could be curtains," I said, thinking I might die in her arms.

She smiled. "Not likely, Kylie."

The grinding, the rolling, the terrifying instability slowly faded. There were a few final tremors, then everything was unnervingly quiet.

I could hear my own breathing, fast and furious.

"Don't be frightened," said Ariana.

"It's not fear," I said.

She gave me a long blue stare.

And then she kissed me.

ABOUT CLAIRE MCNAB

Claire McNab is the author of the Detective Inspector Carol Ashton and the Undercover Agent Denise Cleever series. Like the star of her new series, Kylie Kendall, Claire left her native Australia to live in Los Angeles...a city she still finds quite astonishing.